The Dreidl Disaster

The Dreidl Disaster

A Last Girls Standing Romance

Stacey Agdern

TULE
PUBLISHING

Dedication

This is for:

The Hanukkah Fans,

Those who work behind the scenes to get things done,

and

The Medical professionals who watched over me, and the friends and family who helped me through.

Chapter One

OFF THE CAMPAIGN trail and back to work.

Newly elected member of the County Board of Legislators Olivia Nachman wouldn't have it any other way. She had a spring in her step, a fantastic mix of pumpkin, milk, and java from the Cupcake Stop, and all of her materials prepped and ready as she returned to her seat in the room in town hall where the Briarwood village government held their special committee meetings.

"Welcome back, Liv!"

"Welcome back, Mayor!"

"Congratulations, Mayor Nachman!"

When a group of people used her name and her title interchangeably, Liv knew that she was home. Which, she noted, she was, considering she'd known a large number of people in the room since her childhood.

But more importantly, this particular special committee, which included representatives from the Briarwood Temple Sisterhood, the Interfaith Clergy Council, and the Briarwood Chamber of Commerce, had gathered together for a very important moment; one she'd been looking forward to.

"Thank you, everybody," she said. "What's our agenda for tonight?"

The question, of course, was a formality—always asked by the sitting mayor right before the beginning of the meeting.

"Presentation to the special committee by Flaire Hutton of the New York Empires," said Mark, the longtime Briarwood cameraperson. The man responsible for making these committee meetings accessible to the entire town. "A proposal for the ceremonies and events surrounding the installation of the dreidl sculpture."

"Is Ms. Hutton here?"

A hand was raised, revealing nails that were a blend of red and green and an Empires crest. The young woman wearing the distinctive colors was pale, with straight blonde hair, bright blue eyes and a tiny nose. "Present, your honor," she said. "Uh…honored mayor…"

"Thank you, Ms. Hutton," Liv said, smiling. "I think we're ready." After going through the formalities required of the committee at the beginning of the meeting, it was time. And because she decided to take pity on the young woman, she altered a policy. "Let's save questions for the end."

The young woman nodded, walking to the front of the room, wearing a bright red and green suit and a smile.

"The holiday season is important to the Empires," the young woman began as she settled her materials on the lectern. "And with our donation of a collection of hockey sticks from our recent Men's Hockey League Championship season and their use to create a dray-dell, it is very clear that team is quite interested in celebrating the season with Briarwood."

As the laptop came to life, a schedule was posted on the ancient pulldown screen. Noises Liv could only explain as gasps of horror emanated from some of the participants. She caught some eyes and lowered her hand in the universal gesture for 'quiet.'

"We would begin with a kickoff event on the Friday evening," Flaire continued, whether she was oblivious to the noises or too excited about the presentation to notice, Liv wasn't sure. "We will have a beautiful party, music, and excitement on the grounds of the Briarwood Temple. On Saturday morning, the children of the village will be invited to join the festivities with a beautiful gelt hunt, fun and prizes and festivities on the grounds of the temple. We would continue festivities through the day, continuing with a beautiful, quiet religious ceremony on Sunday, maybe with the pastor or a reverend leading the service with the children from the choir singing, and the dreedell being unveiled after the service, where it will be blessed by all of the clergy from the council."

Flaire paused, as if she was expecting questions before she pressed the laptop again, revealing...a list of food regulations. Another part of the room gasped in horror.

Now it was time for her to say something. "Quiet

down," Liv interjected. "I want to remind everybody that there will be time for questions at the end."

"Thank you, Mayor." Flaire continued, "Part two is the food. Because everybody wants food at a holiday celebration. There would be food everywhere, celebrating the spirit of the season. Healthy baked food, with beautiful symbolic cookies including festive jelly-filled triangle cookies and buttery mataza crackers with salt water and honey with apples to celebrate the miracle of this season."

Once again there was a pause, and more horror came across the screen, as the next group of people reacted to the regulations.

"We would also like to see decorations, of silver and green and red, as well as a blue that matches the Empires color palette; that is the only color that will need to be checked to specifications of course. No non-Empires blue allowed. Flags and beautiful noisemakers should be used on shop windows, in celebration of your festive season and the dreedell."

Liv tamped down her own emotions, looking at the members of this special committee. "Are there any questions?"

There were, as expected, many hands raised.

"Okay. We're going to take these questions topic by topic, to make things a bit more orderly if that's possible?"

There were approving noises from the room, which relieved Liv just a little bit.

And then the questions started.

Reverend Kennedy, the representative from the town's interfaith council, was the first to raise his hand. "Why would you have events on the grounds of the synagogue while there are services going on? There are so many other locations where events could occur."

"Synagogue...services?" Flaire replied with a smile. "Aren't services on Sundays?"

Which begged the question, as far as Liv was concerned, why would a religious service conducted when Flaire thought the Jewish population would be having services, exclude the Jewish residents, considering the holiday being commemorated was a uniquely Jewish one? But the noise in the room disrupted her thoughts, and reminded her of where she was, and more importantly who she was. Which meant she needed to focus on the next hand raised.

Which of course, belonged to Jennifer Cohen. Jennifer was President of the Briarwood Synagogue's Sisterhood, as well as the mother of the Empires player who had initiated all of this.

"I had a brief question, Flaire. I wanted to thank you for organizing all of this," Jennifer Cohen said, looking to Liv as if she was holding back a great deal of stronger emotions. "But exactly where did you come up with the...gelt hunt?"

"Oh, Mrs. Cohen," said Flaire, seemingly oblivious to the fact that if looks could kill, Jennifer Cohen would be murdering her at this exact moment. "Thank you so much for connecting the team with this beautiful town. Hunting for eggs and other sorts of scavenger hunts is one of my favorite things from childhood, and children love finding things, so I thought it would be a wonderful way to celebrate the holiday and have kids finding chocolate."

The expressions on some of the other committee members' faces were even angrier. "I'm going to table this section and move on," Liv said, feeling the sudden rise of temperature in the room "Questions about the food section?"

Of course it was Frank Maricelli who raised his hand. Maricelli, owner of the Pasta Station, was deeply involved in the Chamber of Commerce's restaurant committee. "Where's the oil? My buddy from Rivertown was telling me about the Hanukkah food and that it needs oil?"

"Oil isn't healthy," Flaire replied. "Apples and honey are so much better, as well as the m...a...taza crackers."

The next hand raised belonged to Paul Levitan, the owner of Levitan's Deli. Liv settled in for the comment.

"My wife," Paul began, "makes a whole bunch of cookies for Jewish holidays and I've never heard of jelly-filled triangle cookies before. Can you talk about them?"

Flaire nodded, her eyes wide, and Liv was nervous; Paul Levitan's wife owned the county favorite Caf and Nosh in Hollowville. "They're called something else but they're triangles with filling. They're a very Jewish cookie, and they'd be perfect now."

And as the anger roiled in the group, Liv knew it was

time to cut everything off. "Okay. I think we've covered everything that we can cover now. Flaire, come to my office tomorrow morning and we'll talk further."

OF COURSE THE end of the meeting preceded phone calls and emails from citizens who noticed anything from the horrible graphics of the presentation with the inconsistent lettering on the dreidls, to the contents each of the commenters had picked up.

Liv had made her own decisions, but there were times when she, as mayor, needed to make decisions based on the citizens she represented. And luckily, there were times when the citizenship agreed with her. This was one of them.

"So," Liv said after Flaire had settled in. "The committee has decided to not only reject the proposal but declared that it's unfixable."

"I'm so sorry," said Flaire, before she left the office, and probably the town, at 9:50 for the final time.

As the door closed behind Flaire, Liv moved on, picking up the office phone and started to dial her contact within the Empires organization, the man directly in charge of the junior rep he sent.

Three rings.

"Hello, this is John Stevens."

"John," she said. "Livvy Nachman calling."

"Livvy. Mayor Nachman. Hi," he said. "How are things in Briarwood?"

"Things have gotten out of control and need to be fixed," she said.

"What do you mean? Flaire said she's been enjoying herself in the village." He paused. "She said it's like she's in a HeartPix movie."

"Glad to hear she's been enjoying herself," Livvy said, holding back the snort that desperately wanted to erupt from her nose. "The entire town, including Jennifer and Peter Cohen, feel she's in a HeartPix movie, but not necessarily one that would, say, end up with the joyful presentation of a dreidl made out of hockey sticks."

There was a long pause before Stevens started to speak. She wasn't sure what rendered him speechless, but she'd bet money it was the fact she'd name-dropped Jennifer and Peter Cohen. After all, Jennifer and her husband Peter were the ones Stevens had to impress.

"What's she done now?"

Liv sighed and launched into an explanation of the committee meeting and the fact that the committee had concluded the proposal was not only unacceptable, but also unfixable. "Basically," Liv continued, "the proposal she created, and the way she answered questions about it, displayed a complete lack of knowledge about Judaism and a total disregard for Jewish customs in general, the celebration that we're creating, and the town."

As the silence extended, Liv had a mental image of a drawing sitting in front of Stevens's desk, with a bull's-eye over an image of her face.

In red.

She wondered if the man had simply dropped dead, sitting there holding the phone. And yet, erupting out of nowhere, there was a deep, angry noise. "What would you like me to do, Mayor Nachman?"

This was easy. "Remove Flaire Hutton from this assignment in Briarwood permanently and fix this. You made this mistake; it's your responsibility to smooth the ruffled feathers, not the least of which belong to Jennifer and Peter Cohen."

There wasn't an 'I'll see what I can do,' or a 'we'll see' or any other sort of equivocation. It was, "Yes, Mayor. I'll get back to you as soon as I have a solution in hand."

While Livvy didn't like the lack of definite timing, she liked the certainty in Stevens's voice. She could tie it to the fact that the Cohens were involved, or she could just chalk it up to her insistence. It didn't matter; it was going to be done.

And the cause of the Hanukkah failure was going to be out of Briarwood. For good.

ARTUR RABINOVITCH HAD been back in the States for a

month. The outreach program he'd run with the Mitzvah Alliance in Eastern Europe was set up and running well without him.

"You can come back and help later," Jacob, his friend and erstwhile partner on this project, had told him. "Door's open."

Meddling friends. He had a bunch of them. Five years before, Abe and Leo had yelled at him about how he'd been working too hard, then encouraged him to run with the idea he and Jacob had come up with: on-the-ground resources for people who needed them. It had brought him back to life, stress directed toward something that could make a difference on a global scale.

But now, five years later, he was back in New York. Problems related to his next job and settling back into life were shoved into a box to be dealt with much later.

Now?

He had a fourteen-ounce tube of sour cream in a custom fridge, waiting for him. The garage was cool, and on his knees he could watch the cleanser work on the black spokes of the wheels of his sports car. The cleanser wasn't going to turn purple, like if the wheels of the car were silver, but he was hoping to see...something.

And he had nothing else to do.

Except, of course, pick up the dessert he was bringing to Abe's.

But that wasn't for a while.

Artur hadn't had a day like this in a long time, and he'd planned to enjoy every bit of it. He took a deep breath, looked at the wheels and waited. The timer he'd set was about to go off when his phone rang.

"Hello?"

"Is this Artur Rabinovitch?"

"Yes," he said. "How can I help you?"

"John Stevens. VP, public relations for the New York Empires. How are you?"

He stood up, moved himself and the rag away from the car. There was no way he'd be able to have this conversation while buffing the car.

Empires. Empires.

Artur had intertwined his career with the Empires a few times, the last a brief conversation before he headed off to work for the Mitzvah Alliance. Now that he was back in New York, and only the day before he'd responded to an email that had been burning a hole in his inbox, from someone on John Stevens's staff, setting a meeting for Monday.

Which meant something was fishy. Because nobody randomly asked him how he was, and nobody who wasn't already in a crisis jumped over an already scheduled meeting.

But it wasn't up to him to determine what Stevens wanted. His role at this point was only to listen. So, he did. "I'm fine," he said. "How can I help you?"

"We've got a situation on our hands," the other man

said. "And I know you have a meeting on Monday with HR, but this is…well."

Stevens sounded nervous.

This wasn't just fishy, it was *herring*.

He wasn't going to make Monday's meeting; that calendar date was going to be dust. But all he said was. "Yes?"

"Can you come in? I know it's a lot to ask but…"

And even though he wasn't sure what was going on, he knew he didn't have another alternative if this man was going to be his boss. "Sure," he said. "It's fine."

When he ended the call, he went through the process of rinsing off and then drying off the wheels before heading upstairs, swallowing down some sour cream and trying to figure out what the hell he was about to get into.

Chapter Two

Sunday

G ENERALLY SPEAKING, AS the mayor Liv's time was valuable. Extremely valuable, and after consulting her five planners, two electronic and three paper, on Saturday night, all of them said the same thing.

Nothing.

Which meant the agenda included coffee over the new members' manual for the County Board of Legislators and any other errands she needed to take care of as she started to form her framework for the office she was going to take in January.

But after she'd gotten back from a run and was heading to take a shower, she heard the distinctive ringtone that belonged to her sister. "Hey, Naomi, what's going on?"

"Where are you?"

She blinked. Naomi sounded…strange, as if something was wrong. "Just got home from a run. I'm heading into the shower and then I'm going to spend the rest of the day starting to read the legislators' manual. Why?"

Instead of an immediate answer, there was something

else. A sigh that sat somewhere between disappointed and sympathetic. "You don't rest enough even after that committee meeting from Hades and the election," Naomi began. "This is me reminding you that you need to be at Levitan's Deli, in the next few hours."

Levitan's…

The mayoral part of her brain reminded her of the facts. Levitan's was a kosher-style Jewish delicatessen that had opened in the center of town during her tenure, in the space once occupied by McManus's pub under circumstances nobody talked about. It included a barbecue menu inspired by a chef from Rivertown.

Which wasn't helpful.

Dammit.

And that's when the lightbulb went on. Judith had called a cousins meeting to discuss wedding prep, and the phone call had come in right around the time Flaire had filled her brain, and the Monday night special committee meeting with the horrible, bad, no good Hanukkah event proposal. And Judith's phone call, which had not been followed up by an email, had slipped her mind.

"Dammit," she said.

"You forgot," Naomi replied, sighing again, suddenly organizer and not sister. "Which is why I'll call you again when you need to leave."

"Which," Liv returned with a grin, "is why I love you."

"Shower now," Naomi continued, still in organizer

mode. "Don't let yourself fall into work before I call again without showering and getting ready."

"Right," she said. "I'll organize myself and then dive into the materials."

"Good," Naomi said. "Talk to you soon."

"See you later," Liv replied and she ended the call, resolved not to dive into the manual, but instead headed into the shower.

As ARTUR GOT off the highway at the Briarwood exit, he called his best friend. Abe Neumann had held that position since Artur arrived in Rivertown from Brooklyn when he was in fifth grade. Artur had been a lonely, snot-nosed kid, who got enveloped in the arms of a ridiculous group of friends and gained brothers—Abe and Leo.

"What's up?"

"Going to Briarwood for an assignment," Artur said. "Can I stay with you?"

Because they'd been friends for so long, Abe didn't ask him anything other than, "When are you coming?"

"Later," he said. "I'm doing a walk-through before I meet the mayor tomorrow."

There was a pause. "Good. Meet me for a late lunch."

He raised an eyebrow; meals with Abe were usually a space in front of the stove where problems were spewed like a geyser—his or Abe's, it didn't matter. But out?

What was going on.

"Nu?"

"Finished a stage," Abe replied in what most likely was horribly accented French. "And Chef wants me back to relish the spoils of my work."

Stage. Internship. While Artur had been in Eastern Europe, Abe had been working at different places, learning the restaurant business. He'd get random phone calls where his best friend updated him about the things he'd been learning, and the choices he was making. It kept them close.

"Where?"

"Levitan's."

Levitan's, a Briarwood staple, was the last place Abe had been working. "Busman's holiday?"

"B's out of town, filming upstate. Hanukkah history at a Christmas tree farm," Abe replied, because Abe and his wife Batya were in love and still adorable. "So, it's just us. And yes," his best friend continued because Abe knew him well. "I'll meet you there."

As he ended the call, he felt excited.

Of course, a few hours later, he'd learned one of the most important lessons—never play cards outside without gloves in November. Chess was different; there was time and space to put your hands in your pockets. But cards?

Completely different story. As comfortable in the cold as he was, his hands were a mess and needed warmth stat.

The game was fun; the ten guys who were playing were hilarious. They liked his fortitude but not enough to give him any information about Hanukkah.

A quick stop at the Cupcake Stop gave him warmth in the form of a gelt latte but no information.

He then headed to the comic book shop, where he was starting to see the pattern.

A smile, his food, or service and then nothing when he started to talk. Politeness to the extreme, as if they'd recognized he wasn't local.

Which did something to his insides he wasn't ready to discuss publicly, if ever.

A few more stops: a quick knish, and then the skate shop where he talked about new skates, but was stopped when he mentioned Hanukkah.

Finally, at around three, his phone buzzed, telling him that Abe was on his way. Which meant he headed over to Levitan's.

THANKFULLY, LIV ONLY had to pull herself away from the manual and head to the car when Naomi called later that afternoon, and there was a parking space right near the front of Levitan's private parking lot. She pulled in, and ran toward the restaurant.

Of course, before she went in search of her cousins and

their table, she wondered if she should actually give herself a look in the mirror, maybe stop and...

No.

She was avoiding them, or rather avoiding the prospect of dealing with what her cousins and her sister would say when she arrived.

And that she needed a shield for, which meant her first stop would be the bathroom.

"One sec," she said as she passed Naomi, heading toward the back of the restaurant, past tables and people into the corridor where the happy, boisterous noises from the kitchen emerged.

And made a left, heading toward the bathroom and smacked into...something hard and soft at the same time.

She inhaled sharply, musk and joy rising up her nostrils, and when she looked up, she had to brace herself from the shock of hazel eyes. "I'm sorry," she managed, pulling herself together, trying desperately not to fall into the constantly changing autumn of those eyes, and cheekbones cut like glass.

"It's okay."

She nodded, again, trying not to let herself succumb to...him. "Fine, thank you."

The silence wasn't uncomfortable; it felt dangerous. She couldn't explain or trust the pull he had over her, and she had a mad impulse to kiss him.

"Livvy..."

Naomi. Saved by her sister. "I have to go," she said, though she really didn't want to.

He nodded. "No worries…" he said. "Livvy."

And there wasn't any assumption that he knew who she was in his voice; she was anonymous, which was a gift in itself.

Which meant before she acted on her worst impulses, in a place that was there to remind her why it was a horrible idea, she smiled, turned on her heel and started to follow her sister toward where her cousins were waiting.

STILL SLIGHTLY FLOATING on the scent of the woman he'd bumped into, Artur headed back to the kitchen where Abe was waiting with Paul Levitan, the owner of the restaurant and Abe's mentor for this period of his education.

"Look what the cat dragged back in here," Abe said with a laugh as he entered the room.

"Meow," he replied, grinning. But at the same time, he was doing his best to envelop himself in the smells of the kitchen—the meats in various stages of cooking and preparation. The scents of friends, of home.

"I am absolutely amazed," he said.

"You should be," Abe replied. "Paul is a certified genius."

"Abe gives me too much credit," Paul replied. "And himself too little."

"Same day different speech?" Artur wondered as he ushered some of the smells closer. "Oh yes," he said. "Joy."

"His matzah balls don't sink," Abe proclaimed.

"Well yes," Paul replied. "Baking soda does the trick every time."

"This one," Abe said with a tone Artur knew too well, "is trying to convince me to defile my matzah balls with seltzer."

"He's right," Paul said before Artur could tie words together. "About matzah balls, but not about Briarwood."

"Oh really?" Abe asked.

"Just make sure you don't meander around town to places that aren't interested in talking," Paul replied before Artur had a chance to answer. "This isn't Hollowville or Rivertown where snooping is accepted. This is a place that does not like outsiders looking for information, especially the kind of information you're looking for."

Abe raised an eyebrow, but Artur nodded.

"Which is very good timing," Paul continued, clear in his expression that the message was heard, "not for an interrogation, but instead for eating."

And as Paul brought out the food, Artur found himself wondering what Monday, and the official beginning of his assignment, would bring.

THANKFULLY, NAOMI WAS able to be convinced that Liv

needed a quick refresh, which meant she had a bit more time.

In the small bathroom, Liv took a deep breath and went to work. A splash of cold water on her face followed by a quick reapplication of her makeup and she was able to leave the bathroom, back straight, smile on her face. This was a glitch; it wasn't anything more than that.

Especially considering the walls of the former McManus's pub were there to remind her of past mistakes; even if Levitan's, the current inhabitant of the space between those walls, reminded her of home as much as the table of her cousins and sister did.

"Hello, everybody," Judith, her first cousin and closest to her in age, said as Liv settled into her seat. "Glad we all could make it."

Which was, of course, directed at her.

"I wanted to update everybody on the progress we've made in the last six months."

"You mean," interjected Judith's younger sister Leah, "on your wedding, our love lives, or both?"

Judith laughed but Liv knew the expression.

"So," Judith continued, clearly not giving up control or her agenda, "aside from Leah, does anybody have any exciting romantic developments to discuss?"

In the moment, Liv's heart stopped, knowing that it was possible her sister was going to tell the group about her recent encounter and the very last thing Liv wanted to do was dissect not only the incident but also the reaction. Especially considering how extreme it felt; this was a normal hot guy and she shouldn't be…

"I'm quitting the dating scene completely," Naomi announced out of nowhere. "I have a very demanding job and an extra client that's driving me out of my mind."

Judith snickered, which was a relief, considering the woman was, in fact, Naomi's extra client. "Fine, fine," her cousin said once she composed herself. "Liv?"

And once again, the spotlight of family was on her.

"Liv's busy trying to find us a place to celebrate Hanukkah," Naomi interjected, once again inserting herself. Whatever was going on, she had no idea.

"Which is all well and good," Judith said, "but there's more to life than Hanukkah and office planning."

Liv snorted. "Every time I think about dating someone, I'm reminded that a guy I had feelings for at one point in my life turned a mayoral race into a personal attack. No thank you."

"Not everybody's like him," Judith answered. "You should…"

Liv raised an eyebrow. "Are we here for your wedding or for an optional interrogation?"

"Well," Leah said with a laugh, "considering my love life is professionally intertwined with Judith's wedding, I think maybe both."

"Since our last wedding meeting," Naomi said, "we've

gotten progress on the ketubah, flower girl dresses, we've gotten bridesmaids dresses, I'll deal with the caterer and ceremony design…"

And as her sister ran through the wedding checklist she'd prepared for Judith, Liv found her mind drifting.

Chapter Three

T HE TRAFFIC ON route nine between Rivertown and Briarwood on Monday morning wasn't awful, which meant that by nine thirty, Artur was standing in front of the mayor's door.

It felt…odd. Not like any other assignment he'd done before, not even the moment where he'd offhandedly offered a solution at the inaugural Rivertown latke fry-off a few years before. And that wasn't even an actual assignment.

Nor was his advice taken seriously then. He hoped it would be now.

The door opened with a creaking noise, revealing…

Her.

Mayor Olivia Nachman.

None of the photos he saw during the hours of research he'd spent the weekend doing came close to demonstrating how captivating she was.

She was gorgeous.

Tall, bright eyes, thick gorgeous hair he wanted to run his fingers through…

But she was his contact, the woman in charge of the situation he'd been sent to fix. She was the one he had to make happy so that his actual bosses were happy.

Which meant he had to keep his interactions with her 100,000 percent professional. And completely forget about the fact he knew what it felt like to have her weight against him.

Because of course she was the woman whose scent had run up his nose and distracted him most of the rest of Sunday.

"Good morning," he managed.

"Come in, sit down," she said, beckoning him into the office behind her, moving folders and files off a chair in front of her desk.

"Thank you," he said. "Thank you very much for making time for me this morning."

"I didn't do very much," she said with a laugh that made his insides gooey. "But what I will tell you is that there's a town meeting happening in the next few days, and you're expected to be there."

"Of course," he said as she dropped a folder full of paper on his lap. More reading material. Right. "I intend to be there. What kind of questions do you need me to address?"

"All of them," she said. "Every single one of them. They're coming from people who had a dream, an idea and a hope that the team you're representing crashed quite publicly."

"Right," he said. "An idea very reminiscent of something

someone saw on a HeartPix movie."

"Yep. And unfortunately for you," she said with a grin, "our story begins at the crisis point of that movie. A Hanukkah celebration turned to shambles because someone didn't understand what the holiday was or needed, for that matter."

Interesting.

Olivia Nachman seemed to have a sense of humor. Better and better, and yet so horribly worse all at the same time. "So you expect me to…present like I'm a developer who's trying to convince the town that they'll supply the funds to make the town festival better than it's been in a long time?"

"Right now," she said, "you're the understudy for the corporation who made big promises and ended up giving the town residents less than nothing to celebrate."

Getting a larger picture of the situation and the way Olivia Nachman's mind worked was an asset he was going to use as best he could. Humor, but this was serious. "So," he suggested. "I'm going to be a punching bag or sitting on a bench, waiting to be dropped into a dunk tank."

"Either, both," she replied in a nonchalant manner that did not suggest she was holding back laughter. "But I'd hope nobody brings tomatoes to this meeting."

It was his turn to act like there was no laughter in his arsenal. "No flying fruit. Got it. And no transparent linen shirts either."

There was a bit of a pause between his reply and hers, and he wondered if she was going to get the reference to the famous scene in a literary adaptation.

"Especially considering in this town, sculptures of you would be made in a less...well, comfortable substance than marble," she said.

"Less permanent I'm thinking, right?" He paused, ran a hand through his hair. Reference nailed. "Is there anybody you think I need to talk to in advance of the meeting? Any central heavy hitters who you think need to be spoken to first?"

"You mean any business owners whose feet you haven't stepped on already?"

"Uh…"

Which meant he was sitting and trying to figure out what had gone so, so wrong, before he found himself remembering Paul Levitan's prophetic words.

He was in trouble.

INSTEAD OF THE gorgeous fixer who had walked into her office, the man who she was trying to forget she'd bumped into on Sunday, Liv was now facing a man who had forgotten how to speak. Against all odds, she waited for him to fill it with some...platitude or something.

Nothing.

Which meant she had to take up the agenda. "It seems you don't know the first thing about Briarwood. Your

Sunday travels ring a bell?"

He put his palms out in what seemed to be a gesture of surrender, if not apology, before clasping one hand in the other. "I'm sorry," he said, as if he'd been suddenly reminded of what he'd done. "I tried to do some advance scouting to make the most of my time, and yours, frankly, but it seems I made a mess of things. My apologies."

Ten points for earnestness, but zero for anything else. Which wasn't enough, especially for someone who had to come in and clean a pretty big mess.

He needed to be aware of his surroundings and learn *quickly*. Because this event, this proposal, needed to be successful, without the second individual the Empires had sent having to hold her hand the entire time. "Were you born in a barn or an industrial complex?"

"Excuse me?"

The wording of the question was out of left field, but the subject matter wasn't. She needed to jolt this man into reality and fast. "What kind of city-slick fixer are you that you can't understand the implications of the fact that you're being called in to fix a mess that offended a lot of people?"

He blinked. "My job is to keep things from getting worse."

"And you thought that randomly wandering into a bunch of places without an introduction, and asking about Hanukkah, was the first step toward making a horrible situation better? As opposed to what you actually did, which was to ruffle a few feathers?"

He didn't have an answer.

Of course he didn't. "I'll repeat myself. What kind city-slick fixer are you?"

"Most important parts of my youth were spent in Rivertown."

She couldn't keep her mouth closed even if she'd wanted to. Of all the answers he could have given her, that one was the most shocking, if not surprising. "You're kidding."

He shook his head. "'Fraid not. Bar Mitzvah at Rivertown Hebrew, went to Rivertown High, all of that lovely stuff."

There were no words. None. Anything she wanted to say or could have crashed against each other, spilling random noises and letters just around her tongue. "I just...I don't..."

"Say it," he said with a smile. "Go ahead."

As if she needed his permission.

But for whatever reason, his statement shoved her phrases together, allowing her to find coherence in the space. "You're from three towns over and you're a fixer who can't figure out the mistake of walking into a town and poking a bruise?"

"Only HeartPix movies forget that small towns like Briarwood and Rivertown aren't cut from the same cloth."

And now the man who had an answer for everything was back, which was a good thing despite the fact that the response she wanted to give to this phrase was sharp and unprofessional. Instead, she shoved the stampeding letters back down her throat and went with the question that acted like a dagger. "What?!"

"To them," he began, presumably including her in the group he was separating out, "I mean writers of HeartPix movies and people who wish to see them as real."

"Okay?"

"To *those* people," he said, "small towns are all the same. But growing up in this area, *we* know that Briarwood isn't Hollowville or Rivertown or even Crystal Springs. They're all small towns in arm's distance of the big city, which is also not evil."

Aside from having answers for everything, he had words that blew way past any topic she was thinking about discussing. "What does that have to do with anything?"

He blinked, as if she'd taken him by surprise. "Not for nothing," he finally said, "but you live in Briarwood. You can't assume that the lessons you learn during your misspent youth in one Westchester town are going to help you understand another three towns over. For all that I knew, I'd run into a town gossip absolutely and utterly willing to tell a stranger about the debacle that was the initial Hanukkah presentation."

Which, after she thought about it for a bit, did make sense. She'd ask him about the misspent youth part later. "Fine," she said. "You're a local bumbler who should know better."

"So, what kind of meeting am I being dropped into?"

Back to the meeting, of course. "A special session where you get to listen to the residents tell you what's wrong, and the questions they have will be the sum total of that agenda."

"Right," he said. "Okay. So after yesterday, heck during the depths of this conversation, it's even more obvious that I'm going to need introductions to people, especially the ones whose toes Flaire stepped on the most in the process of creating this festival. And the toes I inadvertently stepped on further by trying to get more information."

"It's not a festival," she said, knowing that it wasn't the answer to the question he wanted, but something she needed to make clear from the very beginning. "This is not Hollowville. We don't have festivals here. We're Briarwood. This is an opening, an installation, showing the beauty of art in Briarwood at Hanukkah time."

"Noted."

"So," she continued, driving the conversation back to his question. "You need introductions from me before you to confront them all at the meeting."

"I'm not confronting anybody," he said.

His tone sounded as if he'd been offended by the concept of confrontation. Which was interesting to her. "Really?"

He nodded. "I'm not going in with my sword drawn. I'm prepared to be marinara."

She blinked; it was all she could manage because she was almost blindsided by his language. Not what he *meant*, but what he said.

"Sorry," he said, sounding tired. "If they bring tomatoes, I'm prepared to be hit."

Which is what she figured; did he sound tired because he was done explaining? So she gave him something. "Falling on a sword instead of going on the attack?"

It was his turn to blink. "Yeah," he finally said. "Better use of my time and the town's. Why defend something I know is wrong? Again. Making things better, not worse."

She nodded. "Okay," she said. "That makes sense."

He smiled, and she wasn't sure why she liked that smile so much. "I'm glad."

"If I tell you I'll help you," she ventured. "What's your plan? With the added idea that my schedule is busy as I'm newly juggling two positions."

"Newly juggling," he said. "I take it you won an election?"

She nodded. "I'm a member of the County Board of Legislators starting in January."

"Congratulations," he said, sounding genuine.

"Thank you," she replied. "So. Anyway, idea? Time crunch?"

"Nothing too drastic," he said, the smile blinding her. "Walk around town, visit the game shop, get a knish or something. See what the climate is like."

"With the added benefit of a public appearance that acts like my endorsement of your mission."

He nodded. "That's the goal."

Of course it was. It was her job after all. And yet all the same, she knew she was going to be stuck. "Prepared to get a latte bath?"

He laughed and for some reason, that laugh unlocked something inside of her glow. "As long as I'm not covered in spoiled milk, I don't mind."

She didn't expect him to get covered in spoiled milk, but as she led him into the hallway, she hoped that she wouldn't be stuck in something she couldn't get herself out of.

ARTUR WOULD NEVER stop being astounded at how quickly and completely the mood of a town could change. Small towns were sometimes insular, but sometimes braced against both internal and external forces. Towns like Briarwood, Hollowville and Rivertown, as far as he knew, were towns that were open and accepting. He'd seen it himself in Rivertown.

Now, here he was, watching the chrysalis of Briarwood he'd seen on Sunday turn into the butterfly he knew it could be. All it took the insertion of one Mayor Livvy Nachman into the equation.

It was beautiful.

This was the Briarwood he needed to learn about, not the one that only the few people who knew his bona fides from outside of Briarwood were willing to share with him the day before.

The mayor stood next to him; her eyes focused. He had to think quickly because she was busy, and he didn't want to lose her attention. "Talk to me about Briarwood."

"So," Mayor Nachman...Liv...replied, "Briarwood has your basic Hudson Valley town structure."

Subtext: just like Rivertown and Hollowville.

"But the Briarwood business improvement district has influenced a bunch of new businesses to set up shop here in Briarwood in the last few years," she continued. "Which means a few new faces have joined the familiar ones. And there has also been an influx of people willing and interested in supporting Briarwood and its businesses."

Which was nice, and probably followed the same pattern Rockliffe Manor had, if he had to guess, considering who now lived here part of the time. However, Artur didn't want a tourist guide, or a discussion about some of the people he suspected were behind the influx of the town's cash. Instead, he wanted her invested in what he was doing, and hearing her talk about Briarwood's future made him think. He wanted to hear more of it. "Do you have a vision?"

He wasn't sure whether she expected him to ask that question, but all the same she took a while to answer it.

"I did," she finally said, gesturing widely as if her hands could hold the whole town. "This is better than I expected after five years, except of course, for the problem the Hanukkah event became."

He smiled. "That's what I'm here to fix. That aside, talk to me about your favorite parts of Briarwood. What's your biggest victory?"

Once again, there was a long pause. "I think if you consider all the things that have happened over the last few years," the mayor continued as if she'd accepted his answer, if not his presence, "I'd say our biggest victory is that Briarwood houses the first branch of Greenblatt's Knish Shop that's opened outside of Manhattan, ever."

Which *was* impressive. He'd visited the store the day before and he'd had tons of thoughts about its origins and how they'd managed it.

None of which were for public consumption.

But he had to keep it cool. "Greenblatt's does bring both good history cred and even better foodie cred to Briarwood."

She nodded. "Yeah. It does."

And there it was. The smile on her face, the brightness in her eyes; he could sit in that moment of pure unadulterated joy with her forever. He was, in fact, a sucker for people who were ridiculously proud of things they'd done.

But he wasn't there to enjoy moments; he was there to work. "Is there anything else you want?"

"Before I leave office, you mean?"

He nodded. "Yeah."

"I want an event that goes off without a hitch. Can you do that for me?"

"I'll make sure it happens," he said. "I promise."

He only hoped that he could manage it…without causing more damage than had already been done.

NOT EVERYBODY WAS Jerry McManus, Liv reminded herself.

But as she told her sister, her life was different because of Jerry. And not just for her, for the people of Briarwood as well. Because Jerry McManus's behavior had turned her life into a fishbowl.

Even as she did something as notable as stand on the sidewalk in front of town hall with Artur, so many people stopped what they were doing in order to…look at her; there was at least one collision at the center of Main Street. There were also at least three 'sorrys' and…at least two people who had to be dragged away from the scene.

But there was one underlying truth: she was cold. She could chalk it up to poor planning, where her fall sweater was not exactly warm enough for the time when fall fought winter's arrival. She could also chalk it up to the fact that she hadn't expected to be out here this long with him. Which meant she had to do something.

"Okay," she said as she shoved her hands into the pockets of the sweater, wishing she'd at least brought her gloves with her. "Let's take a walk."

He nodded, following her onto the street, letting her lead

the way but standing on the outside.

Like a gentleman.

And if she hadn't seen the stares or the sorrys as they were in front of town hall, the stares they got as they were walking through Briarwood would have made her angrier than she was.

But she was with him, in the middle of town. And the residents of Briarwood weren't sure what to make of that. Of course, if she really thought about it, she wasn't either.

But all the same, whether out of political obligation or duty, she had to say something. "They're harmless."

Artur stopped walking, and she wondered what he was thinking. "You're the mayor," he finally said. "Walking with me through a town that didn't want to acknowledge my existence yesterday."

Which was only partly true.

But as they continued their walk through town, she felt an energy in the air. She felt it most as they walked through the town public gardens. "These are maintained by a bunch of different gardening clubs and other organizations," she said, once again electing to be professional in the face of unprofessional things.

"I can see they put a lot of work into this."

The rhododendrons and pines, evergreens and maples, the leaves that decorated the temple sukkah and the boughs that went to at least three churches for wreath making.

She smiled. "They did," she said. "I wasn't here at the

original planting, but I see the maintenance schedule."

If she could put a finger on it, she'd say that the energy of the town felt brand new when she was with him. Not just because she was seeing it through his eyes. Being with him reminded her of the town's history because he might ask questions in his quest to understand.

"Do you know where the sculpture is going to go?"

Shifting gears was easy. Liv had a master's in it, and so she nodded. Despite everything that had happened, the one central thing that started the conversation between Briarwood and the Empires had stayed the same: the large custom sculpture that was being made of the sticks the Empires were supplying. But that wasn't all; the sticks had been used by the players through their recent championship run, including the stick used by Briarwood High School Alumnus Tyler Cohen, to score the decisive goal in the final game.

The sculpture, and the sticks, were the reason why Artur Rabinovitch was standing there, right in front of her.

She stopped thinking about trails and ties and all of the things and took his hand. Liv reminded herself she was taking this hand for business purposes, knowing it was easier to make sure he was following her, and more efficient than saying 'come this way.'

But all the same, she had to brace herself for the impact of his expression. The half confusion, half surprise as his fingers slowly intertwined in hers.

And the warmth of his fingers.

"Come on," she said. Because she had to say it anyway.

"Hold on," he said.

She raised an eyebrow, and as she watched him grip the sides of his jacket, she shook her head. "I'm fine."

"Cold's never been my problem," he said.

"Still don't need your jacket, though I appreciate the offer."

He nodded, and she desperately wanted to take the jacket, but she wasn't going to wear his jacket on a walk through town. So, she tried to ignore how warm he was, how warm his fingers were when he held her hand again. Because otherwise her resolve would fold like a piece of origami paper wielded by an expert.

Finally, they made it through to the center of the square. "Here," she said, "for anybody who wants to see it."

He nodded, looked in the direction she'd been pointing, then let her hand go.

Immediately, without pausing, she shoved her hands in the pockets of her sweater, knowing it wouldn't compensate for the loss of the warmth in his hands.

Focus on something else, she scolded herself.

Of course, her traitorous eyes followed Artur himself, as he walked determinedly around the place where she'd envisioned the sculpture being.

When he returned, he met her eyes and she was absolutely not surprised when he offered her his jacket again, holding it out on long fingers. "Not cold," he said. "You look like an icicle, and it's not professional of me to permit that."

This time, she was powerless to resist. "I'm taking it for professional reasons," she said. "And I accept your offer with a provision to provide you with some kind of warm drink when it's professionally convenient."

"I'll take that under advisement," he said, those eyes twinkling.

She was going to delve into fool territory if she didn't watch herself.

"Speaking of warm drinks," he continued, taking her hand back as if it was nothing, her fingers seeking the warmth of his. "Does the town have an outdoor café during the summer?"

That was a memory. And that was a question she could answer. "We do. Last summer, we got all the businesses together and did an outdoor event in the middle of the square. It's not something we do regularly because the town isn't built for that, but we've been known to do it on special occasions, three-day weekends, holidays."

"I haven't heard anything," he said, "so I don't know the temperature of the village residents, but what about some kind of outdoor gathering space around the dreidl?"

"I like that," she said, walking toward the perimeter of the square. "We'd keep about five chess tables but make the dreidl and the square the center of everything."

"This way you can move the festivities away from the synagogue."

"An added benefit I hadn't thought of," she said, grinning. The wheels were turning in her head, and she couldn't wait to put everything into fruition. "We can also set up a temporary stage and a covering."

"Community space down below," he said. "For community members, community businesses. No outside, not yet. But community businesses and maybe some hot chocolate and..."

"Yes," she said, running along with the visions, whether it was his, hers, or both of theirs. "This is where you sell the hot chocolate; this is where someone brings latkes and handmade gelt. This is where the sweet bimuelos, soofganiyot by the dozen, and the rest of the traditional foods show up. Getting goose bumps."

He smiled. "To get to this stage, what do we have to do?"

"Survive Thursday's meeting."

"And hope nobody brings a guillotine."

She snickered. "No. I don't think it's going to be that bad. Maybe a Hebrew dictionary."

"I could absolutely see that happening. But don't worry," he said, displaying his free hand and putting one finger over the other as if he'd braided them. "Hebrew and I are like that."

"Glad to hear," she said. "But yeah. Thursday."

"And you're in the office tomorrow?"

She nodded. "I've got a pretty packed schedule for the next two days including one of the transition meetings."

"Teaching the new mayor?"

She nodded. "Yes. That's the meeting I have for most of Wednesday. Updating the new mayor on everything and teaching them how Briarwood works—or has for the past five years."

He looked at her, and she wasn't sure what he saw in her expression. "Are you ready to leave Briarwood behind?"

"I'm ready to leave the village politics behind, and I'm ready to try and serve my community on a larger scale, but I'm not leaving Briarwood. I still live here."

He didn't answer immediately, but she saw the thoughts play across his face. "Which is why all of this is important?"

"One of the reasons," she said. "I wanted... I want to leave something behind. I want to celebrate here, in Briarwood, one more time before my focus is taken elsewhere."

He nodded, but he didn't respond immediately. But she could see the flames that made his eyes glow with something she couldn't identify. But when he spoke, it was quiet.

"We'll do this," he said, as if fixing what had been broken was a foregone conclusion, and nothing and nobody would keep him from bringing her vision of community to Briarwood one last time. And for the first time since Artur walked into her office on Monday morning, Liv believed it.

She'd be happier, however, if she could extricate her hand from his.

And if she could give back his jacket.

Chapter Four

THE NEXT MORNING, Artur borrowed one of Abe's old jackets, which didn't fit, and headed over to the Briarwood synagogue in search of information.

A parking space was easy to find, but information was not.

"Rabbi Leibowitz is busy," the temple administrator informed him, taking a break from moving papers around her desk to briefly look him in the eye. "Even though we are not heading toward our busy season, we are heading away from it, and it's as if people have just discovered our existence."

Which Artur could understand.

"Including," the administrator continued, looking up once again, only to push her glasses up her nose, "hockey teams who don't understand the meaning of Shabbas even though they're…attempting to organize an event for the town."

If he was a different person, the barb would have landed. But as he'd come in expecting to fix trouble, not assuming it didn't exist, he smiled. "That's what I'm here to fix."

Clearly unconvinced, she said, "Which is all well and

good, but the schedule is busy and you're not seeing anybody. Until Thursday, at least."

Thursday. At the meeting.

He nodded, understanding the underlying negativity. "Right."

"But," the administrator said, "I do have a note from the rabbi."

That was unexpected. "Oh?"

"Rabbi Leibowitz did receive a note from Rabbi Engel of Rivertown, but he already knew you were a good guy from the virtual presentation you did two years ago about on-the-ground Tzedakah."

The presentation.

He'd been on the ground, hoping he had internet.

But he'd been able to get a signal and talked for a few hours about what he was doing. He'd been exhausted, but it had felt good.

"And," the administrator said, "once you've figured out what you're doing with the event here, the rabbi would love to speak to you. He'll have time next week."

Artur nodded, relieved. "Good."

"You should also expect an invitation from Jennifer Cohen. Jennifer's the member of the sisterhood who brought the idea to the mayor and the team."

He made another note. Jennifer Cohen wasn't just a hockey parent; she was a member of the Briarwood Temple Sisterhood. Like the mayor, Jennifer Cohen was deeply intertwined with this town, and this was a glass ball he couldn't drop.

AFTER A VISIT to the library to look through information about older Briarwood cultural events, Artur discovered it was time for food. His destination of course was Levitan's.

"One," he told the person standing at the door before being directed to the bar/deli counter area. He sat down, took a breath and looked up into Paul Levitan's eyes. He could see the stains on his apron, the glasses and the pen behind his ear.

No wonder why his best friend respected him. This was a professional, if Artur hadn't figured it out on Sunday.

"Artur," he said with a grin. "Good to see you back here again. Do you need some help? Information?"

"Lunch…dinner…something."

Levitan nodded. "Anything in particular?"

He shook his head. "Chef's choice."

"Good choice."

Levitan worked the deli counter like a sushi chef, slicing meats and pounding rye bread strong enough for the smell to waft from behind the counter. "Heavier? Lighter?"

He couldn't ask for sour cream; he didn't want to jeopardize Paul's hard earned meat serving license despite his love for the dairy delicacy. So he made a different choice. "Matzah balls?"

"You got it."

A flick of a switch and within minutes, a window behind the man opened to reveal a steaming bowl.

The soup and sandwich were delivered shortly, and were heaven to his nose.

"You want I should give you advice?"

He laughed. Out came the Yiddishisms. "Sure," he said because he was many things, but a fool wasn't one of them. "Tell me."

"You check the bookstore?"

"For?"

"Information," he replied. "Store's run by my wife's friend. First branch was her passion project after she retired from teaching."

"Really?"

He nodded. "Yep. First store's near my wife's diner in Hollowville; she started this one about maybe *five* years ago."

Hmm. Interesting. He floated the name to confirm it. "Tales from Hollowville is the other one?"

"You catch on quick."

Artur smiled. "Anybody else who's probably open to talking?"

Levitan paused a moment; Artur could see the older man trying to pull the facts into his brain by sheer force. "Italian place. They had trouble a few years ago. They got some help from a place in Rivertown. Nobody knew because everybody was quiet."

Thoughts ran around his head as Levitan shrugged.

"Only reason I know is because they needed someone who'd keep it between them to organize the paperwork."

Because of course, Paul Levitan was an attorney by trade. He fell in love with the restaurant business because of his wife, owner of Hollowville's famous Dairy restaurant. One more word and Levitan would be the subject of Batya's TV show.

"Which," Paul continued, "is how I got the heads-up on this space."

And then his thoughts clicked. Which Italian restaurant did he know in Rivertown that was led by a family tradition of hearts bigger than the world? There could be only one.

"Fratelli's?"

Predictably in the way of small-town gossip chains, Levitan nodded. "That's the place. Anyway, start with the bookstore and then go to the Italian place. That's where you'll get information."

Because of course he was an unknown quantity, but either way, he'd put Leo on a stake later—Leo Fratelli, his other best friend who did not tell him anything.

Now, he had to organize himself, make some notes and hope that Abe would forgive him if he didn't eat much dinner.

Chapter Five

THERE WAS MORE information flow in the transition meeting than Liv remembered from her own meetings with the mayor she succeeded at the beginning of her first term. But time was a strange thing and Terry Fields-Kramer only seemed to have more questions than Liv could answer in two lifetimes, let alone the hours each week she set aside for the transition conversations.

Not to mention every single time Liv would get frustrated, she'd remember how close the beginning of her own Board of Legislators orientation was. The size of the manual and the questions she already had about it were much, much more than the information Terry would have to know.

But there was a knock at the door while she was starting to describe the digitization project she was doing her best to finish. "Come in," she said.

The receptionist at town hall wasn't her secretary, but every once in a while, the kindly gentleman would have to answer the mayor's phone. "Mayor Nachman," Burton Squires said, his typical orange bow tie and matching suspenders brightening the room as he walked into it, "Its

Jennifer Cohen on the line."

"I need to take this," Liv said. Which meant a rapid ending to the meeting, which was par for the course. Except this time, Liv was the one grabbing a phone call and ending a meeting that had already eaten through her allotted lunchtime.

"No worries," Mayor-Elect Fields-Kramer said as she began to gather her things. "I'll see you next week."

Liv felt horrible, but duty called and this time it was calling loudly. After taking a second to compose herself, she answered the call. "Hello, Jennifer, how are you?"

"I'm good, Mayor Nachman," Jennifer said. "Things have been busy here, but I wanted to know how things are proceeding with the fixer."

"Good," she said. "He's surprising. But good."

"Interesting." Jennifer paused, and if the older woman wasn't trying to play matchmaker, Liv would eat her socks. "Peter swears he met the guy a few years ago…maybe at Comic Con when he was running around with one of Tyler's now teammates."

"I can't verify or deny that," Liv replied, "considering I only met the man on Monday. But I can say with reasonable certainty after spending most of Monday with him that he now has a good grasp of what he's been thrown into."

"Very good to hear," Jennifer replied. "The reports I heard from the temple yesterday morning were mixed. But I think that's just Marjorie being Marjorie. They liked him better at the library yesterday."

Marjorie. The temple administrator who acted like she'd been given the kingdom itself, as opposed to just its schedule, at times. "What did Rabbi Leibowitz say?"

"The rabbi was impressed, but is waiting to see what happens at the meeting on Thursday," Jennifer replied.

Which made sense.

"And who did you talk to at the library?"

"Ellen—she's in charge of the information archives in the reference section. She said he was lovely."

"Did she like Flaire?"

"Flaire brought soda into the archives."

Which, if Liv remembered, was a problem for Ellen. "Right."

"Anyway," Jennifer continued, "you sat with him…the fixer on Monday, made sure he understands what he's up against? And the story that needs to be told?"

"He knows the story," she said. "That I can tell you."

"Good," Jennifer replied, sounding slightly mollified. "But I have a more important question."

"Which is?"

"Is there a plan to fix this? Because way too often people tend to have opinions about a situation but not a solution. More importantly than the man himself, does he have a strategy? A plan?"

Jennifer was nervous, and rightfully so. This was the second employee the Empires had sent to facilitate this event, and way too much had gone wrong already.

Liv understood this particular mind-set all too well; it was something that sprinted through her own mind. Which is why she answered the question as well as she could. "His strategy seems to be not to have one," she said. "I will admit it sounds strange, but actually I think it works."

There was a pause. "Interesting."

Good interesting? Bad interesting? She wasn't sure, but there was *something* in Jennifer Cohen's tone that made it clear the other woman wasn't done. "I need to meet him."

It was a reasonable request, and she wondered why the other woman hadn't made it sooner.

"Maybe we can have a meeting," Liv offered. "Town hall, tomorrow before the special session?"

"No," she said. "That's too close, and I need to see if we're going to survive tomorrow's meeting with our dignity intact."

"Fair enough," Liv said, though she believed the other woman was being slightly dramatic despite how high the stakes were for her. "Name the time, and I'll be there."

"What about tonight?"

"What?" It was a surprise, but Liv had to recover quickly. Clearly tomorrow was out of the question so tonight was the best answer. "Here at town hall?"

"No," Jennifer replied.

In the silence that followed, Liv heard finger-nails...Jennifer's or hers or someone's, tapping against a wooden desk.

"I've got an idea," Jennifer broke the silence with a bit of enthusiasm. "How about the two of you come for dinner?"

Once again, Jennifer's solution was…interesting. "Impress him with your potato kugel and then see if you think he's ready?"

Jennifer laughed, but Liv knew there was a degree of confirmation. Liv knew the other woman well enough at this point: temple sisterhood president, friend of the Briarwood synagogue gardening club. She wasn't awful, just…involved.

"Oh I know it's last minute," she continued, as if Liv hadn't said anything, "but having the two of you for dinner would be lovely. Roast beef, yes, maybe some blintzes, but no sour cream…some lovely bread…potato kugel of course."

Which, judging by the tone, was what she'd wanted in the first place. Her, Artur, Peter and Jennifer, eating a menu she'd clearly already planned out. Strategizing or something.

And despite the other plans she'd had to prepare for the meeting, when duty called, she had to answer. "Sure," she said. "Thank you for asking me. I'll be there."

"Good," Jennifer said. "I'd appreciate it if you'd let the fixer know as well; the idea of having his number within Peter's reach is not…something I'd like. You understand."

She did. Peter was a lovely man, not so involved in his son's hockey career as to be a pest, but…someone with enough interest and involvement in things to make Jennifer nervous. "I do," she said. "I absolutely do."

"Good. Looking forward to meeting him and hearing your plans, Mayor."

"Of course," she said, reminding herself who this was. "I'm looking forward to it too."

"Good to hear," Jennifer replied. "See you at seven."

Seven it was. And at seven, she'd show up, bright-eyed and bushy-tailed, ready for anything that could be thrown her way.

Including the fixer she was about to call with a dinner invitation he probably wasn't expecting.

IT WAS COLD in Briarwood. Abe's jacket still wasn't warm enough and thinking of the mayor wearing his jacket was the first step in a slippery slope of dangerously emotional thoughts that would keep Artur off balance.

But there was a larger problem.

His stomach was rumbling, and the friend who, under pressure, had not only promised him lunch but also promised him information was late.

Leo.

He'd known the man since they were ten, and he was trying not chop off his nose to spite his stomach. So as his friend walked toward him, Artur shook his head in admonishment. "I cannot believe I heard about your restaurant's good behavior from someone else."

Leo, of course, shrugged, seemingly unrepentant. "Well if you had told me you needed contacts here, instead of making Abe tell us you were skipping our sacred dinner because you need to prepare to come on an assignment here, I would have mentioned *things*."

He raised an eyebrow. Leo was not cagey, not usually. But this time he was, holding back a bunch of random information and it was absolutely herring. "And if I'd asked, you would have told me you gave Paul Levitan the lead on the deli location?"

Leo shrugged. "Nobody wants that information because nobody in this town likes to mention the very quick demise of McManus's Pub after the last Briarwood mayoral election."

Pay dirt.

What the heck was going on in Briarwood? What was the story with McManus's? But all he said was simply: "What?"

Leo shook his head. "Not here," he said. "We'll talk tomorrow night at dinner. Remind me."

He would, but Leo would probably forget halfway through dinner on Thursday night. Either way, he followed his friend into the Pasta Station.

"Leo…"

And then it was sudden silence as the guy who'd initially greeted Leo so warmly turned slightly. "Him?"

"Stop being a buffoon, Maricelli," Leo said with a shake

of his head. "I've known this guy since he was ten and if you have trouble with him, you have trouble with me."

Which was definitive and weird and...

"But you were with the mayor on Monday. Being...public with her."

Leo raised an eyebrow as scenes from Monday afternoon ran through Artur's head; had the guy who was glaring at him been part of the crowd who stared as he and Liv walked through the square, or was he one of the people who had to be dragged away?

"Am I in fifth grade again or have I walked into an alternative universe?" Leo interjected, incredulous. "The man is *working* with the mayor."

"Artur Rabinovitch," he said, deciding to introduce himself. "Rivertown High Graduate, friend and man hired to fix the mess made of the Hanukkah event here in Briarwood."

The gentleman raised an eyebrow and looked back at Leo. "This guy? This guy is..."

"*The man* is good at his job," Leo said, clearly ready to brawl right in the middle of Briarwood. "And if you're not letting us in, Frank, then I'll just leave and go back to Rivertown."

"No," Frank said, as if he'd suddenly been reminded of the stakes of the situation. "No. I'll reserve my judgment of your friend's job skills until tomorrow's meeting. But now?" he said. "Let me feed you lunch."

And as they headed to the back of the Pasta Station, Artur found himself more curious about McManus's Pub and it's connections to the town, as well as why Frank Maricelli was so concerned about what he'd been doing with Liv...the mayor, on Monday.

LIV CAUGHT A glance of the clock on the wall and groaned at the time when she lifted her head from the pile of work she'd been handling. The time had flown and she needed to make a phone call.

Immediately.

Which meant she had to dig into the email she'd received from John Stevens and the chain that followed, alerting her to Artur's arrival.

Nine numbers, a deep breath and then...

"Artur Rabinovitch."

It sounded like he was in the middle of a wind tunnel, and there were random noises every so often.

Was he going somewhere?

"Hey, it's Liv Nachman," she said. "You sound busy...is this a good time?"

There was a short pause and what sounded like the squeak of a door opening. "It's fine, Mayor," he said. "I'm always busy. How can I help?"

Having found her answer and found herself in the middle of a dead end, she had to push forward. "I just got a call from Jennifer Cohen inviting us to dinner."

There was a long pause and she felt ridiculously guilty about having waited so long to call him; as the pause continued, alarm bells went off in her head. Could he have made other plans?

"Right," he said, cutting through the silence. "I was wondering when they were going to reach out."

Relief. Sweet relief.

He'd been waiting for the call.

"That's what I was thinking when she called me," she said before deciding it was better to make sure. "You good for dinner?"

"Calendar is open," he replied, sounding to her ears as if he'd been smiling. "Anything in particular I should bring?"

This was the tricky part. "Bring a parve dessert. That's what they'll want; they're kosher but they don't talk about it, so don't ask."

"Someone did?"

There wasn't silence, not even a pause. "Yep."

This time there was silence. "What did they say, if you know?"

Explaining this was going to be tricky, but she'd done it at least once before. "Someone said something extolling *traditional* values, or whatever, at some point in front of Peter and Jennifer, in a way that made it obvious they didn't consider keeping kosher in line with those *traditional* values. And so the Cohens continued to keep kosher but stopped talking about it."

"Which is not the solution I'd advise or take," Artur bit out, before pausing again. What was going through his head? Why was he so angry?

"But," he continued, seemingly oblivious to her thoughts, "it's not my house and I wouldn't be the one explaining why I have two sets of everything in my kitchen, separated by different color labels, and don't put butter on my mashed potatoes…to someone who's convinced 'traditional holidays' don't include Yom Kippur, Shabbat, and Passover."

Sore spot. Bad advice given to a Jewish couple. Right.

"Pretty much," she said. But apparently now her goal was to make sure that he didn't ride in with sword drawn for dinner. "Anyway, the damage has been done, so despite the fact the Jewish Hockey Players Association exists and Tyler is involved, they still refuse to admit to being kosher in public."

"Wait," he said, "the head of the JHPA is in Briarwood? Do we want to involve them?"

And that went off the rails for a different reason. Which meant she had to put her foot down. "Whoa," she said. "Once we have a *thing* for the JHPA to be involved in, we can involve the organization. Which means…"

"Right," he said, not even letting her finish but if this was what it took to calm his horses down, she'd let it happen. "Not something that we can discuss till after the meeting tomorrow at least."

"Correct," she said, not even bothering to hide her sigh of relief before directing the conversation back to where it was supposed to be. "Anyway, bring a parve dessert."

"I'll run to a place in Rivertown that has great babka."

She blinked. Of all places, he'd go *there* instead of a place in Briarwood? "Rivertown has babka?"

"Place is tiny," he replied. "It just started selling more than meat last year. Their babka is gold."

And now she got it. "I won't question the babka. Knowing it's coming from a meat place, I won't doubt it's parve."

"Good. What time should I be there?"

"Do you want me to pick you up? I know the area and it can get a little twisty at night."

There was a long silence, and she wondered what was going through his head. Did he want to drive by himself?

"That sounds good," he finally said. "What time?"

She paused a second. "We need to be there by seven, so maybe six thirty?"

"See you at six thirty," he finally said. "Where?"

"My place," she said, a little too quickly for her taste. But then again it was on the way. "I'll give you the address."

"Done," he said, and she heard the sound of his fingers typing on the phone. "Looking forward to it."

And as she ended the call, she realized that she'd have to somehow give him back his jacket.

Chapter Six

A RTUR WASN'T SURE what to do with himself, and he felt like he was missing some information, so before heading over to Geirowitz's to pick up the babka, he called his contact at Empires HQ.

"Emily Gould-Smythe," said an unfamiliar voice. "You're no longer working with John but working with me."

"Good to know," he said considering he was talking with the woman who ran PR at the Empires. "I have a question."

"How can I help?"

"Heading to a dinner hosted by Jennifer and Peter Cohen," he said. "I know Jennifer's background. But is there anything particular about Peter I should know?"

Aside from the fact that he may have run into Peter at an event a number of years before; a one-time job working with Ben Klein at comic con during his rookie season with the Empires in a situation where Empires Captain Chris Emerson had to be out of pocket.

There was a long sigh on Emily's end. Which usually meant either trouble or a difficult to describe situation.

He erred on the side of caution. "Anything I should be

wary of?"

"He's fine," Emily finally said. "He's a fan, a dad, and sometimes blurs the line just a bit. He's made friends on social media with some of the beat reporters, and a bunch of the fans love him. He's a good guy, draws attention to the Empire Bridge Foundation and he makes some noise. Nothing big to worry about."

Translation: Peter Cohen needed to be placated so that he would placate social media, but nothing at all said around him would be private. "Right. I'll be careful."

"Good," she said. "Call me tomorrow with an update?"

He nodded. "Sounds good."

An hour and a bit after he ended the call, babka secured, route nine traffic patterns on his side, he stood on the mayor's front porch; she lived in a town house that reminded him of his place in Brooklyn.

He knocked on the door. "Hi," he said, trying to look at the security camera that seemed to have flashed on. "I'm here."

When she opened the door, he could barely breathe. She was too bright and gorgeous to describe in ways that could fit into a dictionary. Any and all of the languages he knew fell short.

There was simply something special about her.

"I see that," she said, her voice smoldering through the frozen depths of his brain. He tried to focus but he needed all his mental capacity to grab his attention from the dress she wore, one that stole his coherent thought and shoved it through a strainer.

"Do you want to drive or should I?"

It took him a minute for the words to register. "You know the area," he said. "You should drive." Aside from being a smarter suggestion, if she was driving, he didn't have to think about how he'd react to the prospect of her getting into his car…

But he was getting ahead of himself.

He wasn't talking about the sports car that was sitting in the Brooklyn garage. This was a people car; he could have people inside it.

If they followed his rules…

He could.

Eventually. And yet having either gotten no sign of his internal debate, or taken his words at face value, she nodded, stepped past him as if he wasn't even there, and closed the door. "Let's go," she said.

And having been completely shoved out of his element, for the best of reasons, he followed her.

LIV WASN'T SURE how to react to anything. A thrumming in the back of her mind had started when she saw Artur arrive on her doorstep. She almost collapsed at the sight of him on the security camera, looking gorgeous in a way that she hadn't really allowed herself to take notice of since colliding into him in the back hallway of Levitan's.

Why?

Was it because he was standing on her porch like a guy there to take her to dinner...on a date? Or was it just the way the gathering dark of October made him look?

She didn't want to speculate.

It didn't matter because she forced herself away from the dangerous path her thoughts had taken before meeting him at the door and walking to the car.

But those dangerous thoughts had been creeping back in. "You okay?"

His voice yanked her out of the fog she'd been in, long enough to realize she'd stopped at the stoplight much longer than she wanted to; the light in front of her was now a brilliant green.

"Fine," she said as she continued along the route. "Thinking about tonight." Because the last thing she wanted was to discuss the random thrumming-turned-fluttering in her stomach.

With the man who was causing it.

Liv needed to remind herself that she was a woman in her thirties, for God's sake, and not a little girl, prone to fall in love with any man thrown in her path.

Not everybody was Jerry McManus, but her life was forever changed because of him.

"Anything I should know?"

Once again, asking her for information as if he'd taken her words at face value. "No," she said, shoving the conversation back from the underlining slide into the personal. "Just... a normal dinner. They'll want strategy, and they're on our side."

"Our side?"

She smiled; she couldn't help it. Whether or not he'd seen it, she wasn't sure. "The side of organizing the event so it can take place."

"Yes," he said.

She could see his smile in the streetlights.

And she tried not to think about what that smile did to her. It wasn't one of his usual megawatt smiles. It was tentative, soft.

The fact that she could tell the difference between his smiles was distressing her.

"You okay?"

"Still nervous," she said, not explaining where those nerves actually derived from. "But that's normal. Not necessarily something to be concerned about."

He nodded, and she didn't have the time to really analyze what was going on because she was pulling into the driveway.

"Nice decorations."

She laughed. The house was decked out in pure Hanukkah. As per usual, there were blue baubles and a large menorah in the center of the yard, and blue and white lights in the shape of Jewish stars strung across every available surface.

"No dreidls though," she said.

"No dreidls."

She smiled. If she could joke, she could do this.

Just dinner at the Cohens, she reminded herself. And then she opened the door. "Showtime," she said as she got out of the car.

And as if she'd conjured him, he was standing next to her.

"You ready?"

He nodded. "I am," he said. "You?"

And then without any more comments or opportunity to make any ridiculous statements, she headed toward the house, knowing that he was right behind her.

Chapter Seven

ARTUR'S MARBLES HAD just been shot out of position, colliding with each other as he tried to focus on the most important item of the evening: business. He needed to help the mayor placate the Cohens, not let his concentration waver.

Not to mention, the mayor was perfectly capable of doing her job and didn't need him watching over her like a mother hen. Not trying to see if she was nervous, not trying to make silly comments to take her mind off of whatever was…swirling inside there.

And definitely not thinking about what she looked like in his jacket.

Which she wasn't wearing.

Better to focus on the five-second reunion with Peter Cohen, who did remember him from Comic Con and insisted on posing in front of the Chris Emerson signed jersey he'd gotten during an Empire Bridge charity event a few weeks later.

While he was holding a babka.

"But I don't want to completely derail the evening," Peter said after catching his wife's expression. "Go sit, dinner will be ready in a minute."

And it smelled fantastic.

"I have," he said, as he stopped awkwardly by Jennifer on the way to the table, "a babka that I've brought."

"Oh great." Jennifer paused, looking at the babka in his hand as if it was radioactive. "Thank you so much."

Her lips were pursed, and he could read the strained politeness that radiated from her.

And then he remembered.

Kosher.

She didn't know it was kosher. Parve.

"I brought it from Geirowitz's in Rivertown," he replied, giving an explanation she didn't ask for, but needed nonetheless. "They just started selling products in store that aren't meat."

"Oh yes," Jennifer replied visibly relieved. "I love their meat and I really love that they're expanding their repertoire. I've been meaning to try Moshe's wife's baking."

"It's good," he said, glad she got the message. "One of my best friends swears by them, and I swear by this."

"Good," she said, and as she spoke, he could see the invisible tick mark going up on his side.

Meanwhile, the mayor had just emerged from the bathroom, looking radiant, nodding with approval Artur couldn't help but feel inside of him.

LIV HAD RETURNED to the room just in time to see Artur pass the babka off to Jennifer without incident, which was a relief.

So was the dinner; it was relaxed, with good food and great conversation.

Until the break between the salad and the main dish, where Jennifer took a long drink of her wine and looked between her and Artur. "You're probably wondering why I've invited you both here."

Artur looked at her, carefully, and didn't say anything.

Which was smart; she wouldn't have either.

"Smart man," Peter said with a laugh. "Man's probably busy enjoying the break before we dive into the delicious dinner I've made."

"Tomorrow night is the meeting," Jennifer continued, gesturing toward her husband, who nodded before leaving, presumably to get the main course. "I need the two of you to reassure me that we're not going to end up in a public fight over something that is supposed to bring both pride and joy to the community and the town."

And this is what Jennifer was worried about.

She didn't want a bloodbath in town hall. She didn't want the connection she'd offered with the Empires, her son's team, to be shattered and broken before the people who'd been chosen to mend the fences had even had a chance to start.

"It's in nobody's best interest to come searching for a fight," Livvy said, after taking a moment to formulate a statement. "Especially if the idea is to be working together and creating something big."

"But it's got to be important to defend the team you represent?"

This last came from Peter as he put the cutting board filled with perfectly cut slices of London broil down on the center of the table. Liv could barely concentrate but she knew the question he'd asked was directed at Artur. Of course, she had no idea what he was going to say; at least he was too focused on dinner to respond immediately.

That, or more likely Peter's words were swirling around Artur's head as he took in the amazing smell of the dinner to come. Because as she spent time with the man, she was starting to realize that he was censoring himself.

She wondered what he'd say if he didn't think about it first.

"I wouldn't be here," he finally said, "if the team's representative hadn't screwed up enough where they needed someone to fix the mess. I'm here to fix the mess, not defend the team or its employees."

Which by this point didn't surprise her. He'd talked about marinara and lattes before; he was just confirming he was ready to take whatever the town threw at him.

"I'm glad you're here to fix what was broken," she began

before turning to the Cohens, trying not to catch a glimpse of whatever expression had perched on Artur's face. "We've had some interesting conversations over the past few days, and I want to make sure you know he has my support."

Jennifer nodded, and the relief was clear in her shoulders and the look on her face. "I'm glad you think so, Mayor…Liv. Things have been difficult over this, and I want to make sure they're going to be smoother moving forward."

"I think this situation is not as dire as you think it is."

"Which is a good thing too." Jennifer looked back and forth as she served herself some slices of meat. "It's a dicey business when the community finds itself at odds with the rest of the town."

Liv understood the concerns. The Jewish community in a small town was a community of its own, and its relations with the larger community could go from good to bad in seconds. Especially over an event that wasn't the easiest to organize, or even persuade the town to have.

"Thankfully," Liv replied. "For everybody's sake, as large as things have gotten, it's mostly an intra-community dispute. Most of the problems stem from the content, not the subject of the event."

Now she caught a glimpse of Artur's expression, in the slight lift of his eyebrows. "No opportunistic locusts with beards coming to plant decorated trees where they don't belong?"

Liv bit her lip to keep from laughing.

But now she understood.

This was why Artur censored himself; if he didn't think, didn't rephrase what he was going to say before he let it out, *this* was what would come out. Glib and descriptive sentences that mixed metaphors better than the original and bypassed rules that suddenly didn't apply.

His uncensored dialogue lit up a conversation brighter than a shammash and struck right at the center of a point.

If someone was willing to unravel the web his words wove.

But she knew.

She understood.

And she was about to respond when the man himself shook his head, a slight blush on his cheeks.

"Sorry," he said. "I'm glad this dispute over content hasn't been hijacked by those with concerns over subject matter."

"No," Liv said, rushing in to keep the conversation on an even keel. "People have been pretty good. But my guess is that it's not all altruistic. The residents see Hollowville and Rivertown with successful Hanukkah events, and as much as Briarwood residents would like to think they're not influenced by any of the other towns in the Hudson Valley, they're influenced by the popularity of their events. They want a piece of the gelt themselves."

"Good." Peter nodded, satisfied, which made Liv sigh in relief. But she couldn't help but notice the smile that appeared on Artur's face for a brief second before it was erased, as if it had never been there.

ARTUR STOOD UP and walked the length of the dining room toward the place where their hosts had decided to set up the coffee and dessert before heading off to…

Prepare.

Out of the corner of his eye, he saw them.

Blintzes.

Sweet dessert blintzes made parve without sour cream, placed just next to the babka.

His fingers twitched, reaching for the sour cream he usually carried with him. The worst time to reveal a culinary obsession was absolutely when someone you wanted to make a good professional impression on was watching you, so he shoved his fingers in his pocket, hoping nobody would notice.

Thankfully, there was no sour cream in his pocket; after learning the Cohens kept a kosher home, he'd left the tubes in his car, locked in that special fridge Jacob and Abe had gotten him.

And yet what he wouldn't give for a mouthful.

"Hey."

The mayor's voice ripped through his concentration; suddenly his concerns about the food were gone, suddenly his focus was on her. And whether it was the light or the concern in her expression, he could barely gather enough words together to speak. "Yes?"

"Can we talk?"

There were a billion things she could possibly want to discuss, and hopefully none of them had to do with condiments or sports cars.

And other more personal items.

Business. Business.

"Sure," he said. "But at the same time—" he gestured toward the hallway where their hosts had vanished earlier "—is it not a good time?"

"I think they're prepping a bit longer for dessert to make sure we do, you know, talk."

"Like they think we need help getting on the same page or something?"

She nodded, and he wondered why she was blushing. But all the same, he let her lead him to a closed porch area, then waited as she turned toward him. "You had a look on your face."

Did she see his expression when he saw the dessert table? He shoved the concern down his throat, raising an eyebrow and going for as nonchalant as he could manage. "What look? It's my face."

"No," she said, a tinge of laughter broadening her tone. "I've seen your face before. That was a look."

Right. Okay. She saw something. He shrugged. "It's

nothing."

Confusion and a little bit of…not full surprise, but *something* he couldn't define emerged from the depths of her eyes. "You went from denying it was a look to saying it was nothing. Can't be nothing."

"I'll tell you later," he said, hoping she'd forget it but knowing she'd be like a counter-surfing dog who just scented the dinner leftovers within her reach.

Chapter Eight

THERE WAS SOMETHING going on with Artur; it was the expression on his face when Liv saw him standing in front of the dessert table, that tension in his shoulders she wasn't ready to admit to herself that she recognized.

What about that dessert table made him so tense?

He'd refused to discuss it when she brought him outside, whatever compelled her to go in search of him to discuss gone completely. He gave her some random answer, but she'd been around enough people to know that he was actually engaging in the kind of 'I don't want to talk about this now' conversation that really meant 'I hope you forget we had this conversation.'

But whatever it was disappeared when they came back to dessert; the babka took center stage and the Cohens seemed…a bit more relaxed.

Of course once she got him in the car, there was another thing to talk about. Professionalism first. "So," she said. "How do you think dinner went?"

"Good," he said as he settled into his seat. "I think the Cohens are ready for what's going to happen. More importantly, they trust that you and I will be ready to handle tomorrow's meeting."

"That's what I thought too," she said. "The power of babka."

She could see his smile just out of the corner of her eye.

"Yes," he said. "Babka and pure understanding."

"What do you mean?"

He sighed, and she wondered what was going through his head; did it have to do with his expression and the tension at the dessert table?

"The Cohens were treated horribly by a previous PR person," he said. "You know it bothers me. They were set up for interviews and conversations, because Tyler's a superstar, but the person wasn't sensitive."

"Right." Didn't they have this conversation already?

"Anyway," he continued, as if she hadn't said anything, "there's a difference between following someone's house rules and understanding them. I brought a parve babka from a meat shop and didn't ask for sour cream with the blintzes. I didn't even carry sour cream because…"

"You know the Cohens are sensitive."

There wasn't an immediate response, but in the darkness when they were stopped at the light, she heard at soft "Yeah."

"So the table?"

He laughed, and she wished she could see the expression on his face. "Yeah. Feelings."

"About the sour cream?" she asked, just wanting to make sure.

"Some people have cigars; others have sour cream. I'd say it was an emotional support condiment, but I think it's more than that."

"My sister has pickles," she finally said, not knowing whether Naomi had gotten over the pickle obsession. "Which is not exactly secret but not exactly open either."

"Do you have one?"

Not a food one, but she wasn't going to tell him about her figurines just yet. "I don't. I just keep track of everybody else's."

"And you don't have a question?"

There was something about the tone, the words…something, that made her not just randomly dismiss it. Surprise that she understood? Surprise that she didn't react?

It didn't matter. "If I didn't question my sister and her need for everything pickle," she said as clearly and as carefully as she could, "I wouldn't question your sour cream."

And when she made the turn into her development, she realized she'd never been so upset to be home in her lifetime.

Thursday was going to be ridiculously busy: strategy session upon strategy session, and then the meeting itself. Yet despite all of that, and how much of a horrible idea it was going to be, she didn't want the night to end.

As she pulled into her driveway, she had an idea.

"Your jacket," she said. "I need to get it for you. Do you want to come in while I get it?"

"Are you sure?"

She nodded. "Yes. I'll even throw in one of those warm drinks I owe you."

"Then," he said, "I'll take you up on it."

Of course, she had no idea what she was doing, but she was going to figure it out.

"NOW THAT YOU have me here," Artur said with a laugh, as he walked into the Mayor's house, "what are you going to do with me?"

Liv snickered. "I'm not going to show you my etchings if that's what you're asking."

"As long as you don't intend to feed me applesauce, we're okay…" And then he realized what he was saying and to whom before he stopped. "I'm sorry," he managed. "I…"

"It's fine," she said. "I like the way you sound when you don't censor yourself…"

She didn't just stop talking; she covered her mouth with her hand.

"Are you okay?"

"I don't know what's going on," she said. "And…"

"And what?"

She sighed, gesturing toward the couch. "My life is complex, and people don't usually get it. And because of the...goals I have, I'm even more careful about what I do and who I spend time with. And what that might mean."

Those were words he understood. "I deal with...scandals regularly," he said, glad his job was what it was, "so I have an idea of the pressure you might be under. Don't want you to end up covered in tomatoes."

The expression on her face fascinated him; she clearly didn't want to laugh but it was obvious she had no choice.

"But at the same time," he said, walking toward the couch, stopping in front of her, gesturing toward the space between them, "I'm not sure what's going on, what's between us. But I'm sure that whatever this is, it doesn't happen every day. To me...ever, really."

The silence that lapsed between them was going to choke him. When someone like her even remotely expressed vulnerability? That was it.

Because that kind of behavior from someone so strong led to protective instincts, which had already reared to life within him.

"So," she asked. "What do you suggest? How do we deal with this?"

"Blame the starlight; heck, blame the sour cream."

And when she put her head on his shoulder, he reached his arm around her and pulled her close, ran his fingers through her hair.

It was comfortable, more than comfortable; just like his

jacket when she eventually gave it back to him, covered in her scent. It would take every single inch of strength he had to actually put the jacket on and not turn it into an air freshener.

Chapter Nine

L IV BARELY MANAGED to make it out the door and to town hall before her phone rang. "Hello?"

"So you were showing the fixer around town?"

Judith. Of course. Her meddling first cousin. And even though Liv desperately wanted to snap, Judith deserved to be answered. "I was doing my job. Don't you have a wedding to plan?"

"My wedding is being planned," Judith replied with a laugh. "But what about the jacket?"

Liv blinked. "What about the jacket?"

"You were wearing a jacket that was significantly larger…"

"It was cold, I didn't bring one," she said, annoyed that this conversation was even happening. She'd reluctantly returned the jacket to Artur the night before, and having made the mistake of almost kissing him.

Mistake.

Not to mention, she'd been in public wearing Artur's Jacket on MONDAY. This was three days later. And not everybody was Jerry McManus. However, the whole

McManus incident had exploited the bad side of being a single woman, who was also the mayor of the small town she grew up in. Everywhere she went, there were eyes.

Ugh.

But the worst part of it was the fact that her trustable, dependable cousin was asking these questions. Judith had been a lock box for secrets and advice for years. But since she drank the Kool-Aid about relationships and got deeper into Briarwood circles, her cousin had changed. "Is this middle school?"

"You're the mayor," Judith said. "He's the fixer who been sent to clean up the very public mess made by the people who are employing him. Who apparently made waves in town the day before you took your very public walk."

Now it was time for the reality check. "Have you decided to become a town gossip in your spare time?"

"No," Judith replied, as nonchalantly as possible, except for the fact that something in her cousin's tone told Liv she wasn't done speaking. "I'm marrying him."

Which made sense. Ash, her fiancé, was personable; everybody loved him, and he had chosen to spend his post-hockey-playing life in Briarwood, including basing his foundation and mentorship program in the town's business improvement district. Of course, some of the town gossip had started to flow his way.

Just to be sure, she needed to know what her cousin's future husband had been told. "So he put you up to this?"

"Not so much put me up," Judith said, "but more specifically, asked me to ask you a few questions when I spoke to you."

She shook her head. "Why didn't he just call me?"

"Who knows," Judith sighed. "But I think he didn't want anything to be considered formal or directly coming from him until, you know, some kind of formal conversation."

She blinked, but then again people were sometimes weird that way with her. Talking with her about town projects was either a conversation that was exciting or fearful, where people didn't want to get signed up to help with something or couldn't wait to tell her how they wanted to get involved.

It was a balancing act for sure. Which is why Ash was using Judith as a messenger or go-between. All the same she wanted to know what was going on. "What did he say?"

"He wanted to know three things."

"Three?"

She was ridiculously proud of not making the Passover joke she wanted to.

"Four questions are now our little hockey playing niece Ramona's responsibility now, because I could hear the hesitation."

Liv snickered; the four questions were always the responsibility of the youngest person at the Passover seder and that had been the perfect joke. Which is why Judith didn't let the opportunity slip to make it even if Liv had. But time was precious, and she knew that questions were coming even if she didn't want them to. "Come on already; ask because I need to leave."

"Fine," Judith said, "Ash wanted to know what kind of guy he was and whether you wanted him involved in the situation on the immediate level or the Hanukkah event in general."

Which was something she and Artur had spoken about, but Judith didn't need to know that. "About the latter, I'll let him know when I need him; about the former, he's a good guy I think. But I take it someone approached him?"

"No," Judith said. "You can come over and ask him yourself about the gossip at the Cupcake Stop tonight. Come for dinner."

And that's what Judith really wanted. And because it made sense, Liv said, "Sure."

ARTUR WAS EXHAUSTED on meeting day. He'd blame his tiredness on the fact that he hadn't wanted to leave Liv the night before. Not to mention, the main character in the hybrid dream/nightmare he was having was the jacket that sat on the couch. Usually he'd throw it on without a thought as he headed out.

But now?

He wanted to treat it like a pickle.

Sweet, beloved. Preserved just as it was.

Nope.

It was absolutely ridiculous to treat a warm, comfortable jacket he'd had for millennia like a cucumber.

Forcing himself to put on the jacket and NOT focus on how much like Liv it smelled, he took another visit to the library's media center. He found an empty station and cued up the footage of special sessions taken from the local cable stations, notebook and coffee in hand. After he'd watched hours of footage, he had copious notes and a game plan.

Next, in search of lunch and conversation, he took Paul Levitan's advice and called Briarwood Tales to see if Carol, the owner, was there.

Luckily, she was in the store, and over more coffee and a sandwich, she informed him that he had her support. "Just so you know," she'd said, "this is a great place to strategize for things if you need the space. And, some of my best people know how to throw a really good Hanukkah party."

Which was the reminder that he had to ask Batya for Sarah's information. If he was going to go and fix a Hanukkah event, it behooved him to have the number of the person who made them a part of life in the Hudson Valley. And that was Batya's friend Sarah.

Speaking of friends, he also needed to poke Leo about the drama surrounding McManus's Pub...

"And the sculptor..."

Had he turned out for a second? Had she moved on to a conversation about something else? "Wait…what?"

"The guy who's making this dreidl. Max Ellison."

Right. Which made sense; granted he still wondered how Carol got the information when he hadn't gotten it yet. But all he said was, "Okay?"

"Anyway," Carol continued, as an entire dish of sour cream arrived. "My friend in Hollowville has an art gallery and she's met this guy. Weird. Not like Sarah's Isaac—who, by the way, is not only a brilliant metal Sculptor, he's also working in wood these days."

"Can I have her number? The gallery owner?" he asked, aware he needed to check all sources and information when he was prepping to fix trouble.

"Absolutely."

Shortly thereafter, Carol left to take care of other business in the store. "Make yourself at home," she'd said.

After browsing the comic section for a signed copy of one of the new Mr. Shadow origin books, he came back to the café area and called Molly Concannon, owner of the Hollowville art gallery.

"Yeah," Molly said after he'd introduced himself, explained who'd sent him and what he was after, "if you had the number of someone who could possibly fix the sculpture, it would be a good thing."

He blinked. "Why? What's wrong with the sculptor or his art?"

"Max Ellison is a nice guy," she confirmed. "Very talented. But the man wouldn't know a good adhesive if it hit him in the face. A breath of air would knock it down."

Another reason to get Sarah's number from Batya; Hanukkah consultations and access to someone who might step in and fix the dreidl if there was an emergency…in one place.

And when he ended the call, he headed out to his car.

But there were still questions to ask and answer; on the way back to Rivertown, he called Emily Gould-Smythe. After he told her what he'd found and what he'd planned to do, she reassured him that the Empires were willing to follow his lead. "That's why we hired you," she said. "Whatever you say, whatever you organize, we will do."

"Good to hear," he said.

"Let us know how tonight goes; we can strategize from that point."

"Will do," he said as he pulled into the parking lot of Geirowitz's kosher mart, the home of what was becoming his favorite babka. And the key to dinner at Abe's.

Chapter Ten

Dinner at Judith's was the perfect way to take the temperature of the town in the hours before the town meeting. Now that the conversation about the public walk with Artur had finished, Judith and Ash were a friendly source of town gossip.

Not to mention, talking with Artur had made her think about a few things; primarily how ridiculous it was that Asher, as the head of the JHPA, hadn't been involved in any of the 'event' planning previously. Neither by the town nor by the team.

His former team.

Which seemed to bother him a lot less than it would her. But once they were sitting down to dinner, she turned to him. "Would you be willing to work with the town?"

"Of course," Ash said as he took a slice of the taco casserole, the vegan sour cream sitting just off to the side on his plate. "Definitely. Personally and in my capacity as the JHPA founder."

"Good," she said digging into her own piece, sour cream and salsa sitting happy on her plate. "Good to know for the future as things are coming together. I think the Empires are dedicated to making this work."

"Seems so," Ash said. "Fixer seems really focused on getting things together."

"So," Judith interjected. "What's the story with the fixer?"

What Judith meant was: 'you've been talking about this fixer for a while, and I know nothing about him.'

"Artur Rabinovitch," Liv replied, deciding to start with the basics. "He's a good guy."

"He is," Ash said. "Name sounds familiar."

"Oh?"

Ash nodded. "He might be a friend of a mutual friend."

And Liv clearly did not miss the glance that Ash gave Judith. The one that usually meant 'he's friends with Judith's boss who also happened to be Ash's mentor and co-conspirator.'

"So," Judith clarified for Liv's benefit, "is he the one my boss recommended? You know, to Leah when she was looking for a crisis PR person to recommend on behalf of a client of hers?"

Apparently the only way to answer that mess of connection was "Yes?"

"I see," Ash said. "Speaking of connections, do you still want to come and speak at the mentorship program?"

Which was both a merciful change of subject and a reminder. Liv had offered to speak at the holiday party for the mentorship program Ash and *his* mentor were running for high school kids. As someone who spent a lot of time doing community service, she felt it was important for kids to see the impact local government made. "Absolutely," she said. "Give me a date so I can block off the time."

"Excellent," Ash said. "Though I wonder…"

"What?"

"Maybe the kids from the program can participate in the event too, you know, some active examples of community service somehow…"

Liv's mind was suddenly going a million miles a minute—including the kids from the mentorship program would be a way of showing more community involvement in the Hanukkah event.

But also aside from the preliminary conversation with Artur, nobody actually knew what this event, opening…thing would look like. There were also so many different levels to the project, so many questions that needed to be answered…

"Whoa," her project manager cousin said with a smile, most likely recognizing the combined deer in headlights/excitement-filled expression that had made its way onto her face. "I'm sure Liv thinks that's a wonderful idea, but us…Liv…those of us on the side of good, need to get through this meeting tonight. Once that's clear, I'm sure she's got a bunch of moving parts to manage before deciding what kind of role she'd want both you and the kids from the program to take."

"Yes," Liv said, a huge sigh of relief whooshing out of her. "Exactly. Thank you, Ash, for even thinking of the idea. But yes, Judith, you have it exactly. I've got a ton of moving parts that I'm working with, including how the town is going to be feeling after tonight's meeting."

"Or how the fixer of yours is going to handle a large percentage of seven thousand angry Briarwood residents."

"Mine?" Liv managed. "Considering the whole beginning of the conversation was about the ton of connections this guy has to both of you?"

"You did get seen by about…at least half the town walking with him," Ash began, "after the whole incident with McManus turned everybody into protective watchdogs."

And of course, as half her family reminded her that not everybody was McManus, the other used him as a cautionary tale.

For once in her life, she didn't want to engage in this conversation, either side of it. "I think I need to head out," she said.

"Are you sure?" Judith gestured at Liv's plate, which thankfully was clear. "Do you want dessert or leftovers?"

"No," Liv said. "Leftovers are going to need to go in the fridge. I'll be fine. And dessert is probably not a good idea for me tonight."

Judith nodded.

"You need us to come tonight?"

Liv shook her head at Ash's question. "No," she said. "I'll keep you posted."

Somehow, Liv managed to leave her cousin's house, knowing all too well she would have to update Judith and Asher later. But it didn't matter because there were more pressing matters to attend to.

In order to build something, she had to make sure there was a foundation. And the meeting couldn't destroy the tiny little foundation she'd begun to create. Her legacy depended on it.

ARTUR PULLED INTO Abe's driveway, parked on his parking pad, headed up to the front door and walked right in. "Hello?"

Laughter came from the table, Leo and his wife Sapna, Abe and Batya, waiting for him. Friendship and food at its best, he decided.

"What's for dinner?"

"Don't think I'll let you have any if you didn't bring dessert..."

For effect, he lifted the paper bag holding the babka, being careful not to destroy it. "Have dessert, will travel," he said, smiling as he opened the door to put his coat away. "I didn't get the wine but there was a meeting."

"There's always a meeting," Batya.

"So," Artur said as he turned toward Leo, "you have something to tell me."

"About how Briarwood's last campaign for mayor ended up in a gossip ring, which annoyed the Chamber of Commerce enough where they basically forced a longstanding business to not only close, but the family to leave town?"

Artur blinked. "What?"

"You're kidding," Batya said. "That is ridiculous."

"Nope." Leo sat back and told the story, explaining how the candidates and the story shook Briarwood. "But as a result, you have a pack of Dobermans ready to pounce on anybody who comes anywhere near the mayor."

Which was a wild bit of information to digest.

Thankfully there was dairy and a ton of sour cream in all areas of the dinner table. He adored his friends.

And when dinner was done and he and Leo were bringing dishes to the counter by the dishwasher, he asked, "So the money was?"

"Frank Maricelli's contribution to the *get McManus out of town* plan. Paul Levitan did the deal and in exchange, when McManus's was fully empty…"

"Levitan was offered the space."

Leo nodded. "Bingo."

Which was a ton more information to digest than he'd expected. Thankfully, there was the babka and coffee and minutes for him to compose himself. But when they finished and it was time for him to head off to the meeting, Abe and

Sapna arguing about dishes, Batya walked him to the door.

"What's up?" he asked, because of course there was something on her mind; it was obvious. He knew body language too well, and he'd known her since high school.

"You sure you don't want us to come with you?" Batya asked, grinning up at him.

He raised an eyebrow. "You voluntarily would come to this 'kill the rabbit' town meeting in Briarwood on a Thursday night when you'd rather be watching the Legends?"

Batya shrugged. "Hockey can wait. I can sand down a pitchfork with the best of them. Not to mention, meetings or auditions in a high school auditorium sometimes need supporters."

Of course she remembered that day all those years ago, when he and Leo went to support her. "I appreciate it, but I think this needs to be a solo event."

"See that's the thing," she said. "Because I thought standing up in front of an entire audience and confronting ridiculous amounts of stage fright, in order to audition in an auditorium you thought you'd left for the last time ages before, was a solo event. But some people decided otherwise."

"This is different," he said. "I need to hear what's wrong, and if I have people spinning noisemakers to drown out every speaker who finds fault with something done by the company I'm representing, I'll be the villain in the story, not the brave knight who has come to save the day."

Batya snickered, knowing him well enough to figure out he was trying not to become the villain of Briarwood's holiday story. "Right. Nobody needs a sour-cream-flavored hamantaschen," she said, choosing the right dessert metaphor to match the Purim metaphors he'd chosen.

"Not even me," he said with a laugh. "But I appreciate it."

"Good," she said. "Keep me posted, and be careful."

He raised an eyebrow. "I'm not following?"

"It's a bit of a minefield there," Leo said, joining the conversation as usual. "You're being watched like rooster coming into the henhouse. Just...whatever you do, as Batya said, be careful and make good choices, hm?"

"I'll have coffee waiting tomorrow morning," Batya said, "as long as you update me."

Hints taken, he headed out, carrying some sour cream and soofganiyot stolen from the dessert box.

This was going to be an interesting night.

Chapter Eleven

L IV NEEDED TO admit she was concerned about the meeting; whether it was actually the meeting she was concerned about or how the residents would react to the prospect of having the opportunity to yell at the fixer, she couldn't decide.

The fixer.

Not *her* fixer.

No matter what had been said at her town house the night before.

Of course as she headed down Ash and Judith's driveway, she checked her email and saw a message from Burton Squires. Subject was ***emergency***, and in his very typical language, he informed her that: *the 'Special Session of the Briarwood Town Board' had become an event larger than town hall could hold and is now being held at Briarwood High School.*

Many people wanted to participate. Which was fine.

But that wasn't all. Liv went on to read:

I should warn you that something is brewing. There are concerns about the fixer that derive from the Chamber of Commerce; they seem to feel his motives aren't correct and wish to discuss it with him. In person.

Which…

There were many thoughts she had, but there was nothing she could do. Except to call him.

Him…the fixer.

Artur.

Instead of dialing, she searched through her calls list to a number she'd called with a 917 area code.

Three rings.

"Hello?" he said. "Artur Rabinovitch speaking."

He was driving; she could hear the telltale sound of the road. "Mayor Nachman," she said. "Where are you right now?"

"Route nine," he replied. "Between Rivertown and Briarwood, closer to the Briarwood side of it; I'm through Hollowville, heading into North Hollowville. What's going on?"

Relief filled her; he wasn't that far away, thankfully. "I want to make sure you come to Briarwood High School's back parking lot."

There was a long pause, and she wanted to know what he was thinking. "Any particular part of the lot?"

He didn't sound shaken or thrown off by the change of location. "Just pull as close as you can to the building."

"I can do that." And then the silence. "Any particular reason why?"

She decided to give him the barest piece of basic information. "It's probably easier for you to get to the auditorium from the back parking lot. The campus is a bit confusing," she replied. "So I'm sending you to the closest lot."

Not to mention, his car was flashy enough to be noticed; the last thing she wanted was egg all over some expensive paint job.

"Sounds good."

He didn't question her; she wasn't used to that. "You should also be prepared for the fact that the list of people wanting to speak about the festival is not only longer than the town hall could accommodate comfortably but is also steadily growing."

"Okay." She thought he was done, but then he spoke again. "I expected there would be a great deal; things were bad enough for me to come in here in the first place, not to mention the reactions of people when they saw me in town by myself. I'll be there shortly."

And when he ended the call, she didn't feel reassured. She felt nervous, not for herself, but for him.

Why?

He was a grown man who did this for a living. She'd researched him; she'd even spent time with the man, and she was able to tell he was damn good at what he did.

Why did she want to shield him? He wasn't an innocent little thing that needed her protection.

And yet all the same, she found herself wanting desperately to give it to him.

ARTUR WAS NOT surprised when Liv met him at his car. She'd already given the signs of 'there lies danger' at this meeting. Which meant she was going to play bodyguard.

He'd actually worry if the local police or someone wearing protective armor had showed up to actually *be* a bodyguard, but now? It was enough that she was worried; two sets of worries would upset the applecart and then there really would be trouble.

But all the same, he followed the mayor into the night, then into the building, down the hallways to a small room with a desk and bulletin boards where there were instructions on how to apply stage makeup.

He'd wondered where the saws used by the prop makers were; tension in the room was thick enough to create sawdust on the floor. The mayor was pacing and he was about to get whiplash.

"The plan is that they're going to read their complaints out loud, and I'm going to respond to each of them?" he said in an attempt to demonstrate that he was more prepared for what was coming than she expected.

"Traditionally," she said, her words forcibly in place and not shaking all over. "That's how it goes."

And yet she was framing the statement like it was a choice. "That's fine with me," he said, just to make things clear. "We don't need to make any special arrangements for my sake."

She blinked, as if his words were covered in bedsheets with badly cut out eyes. "You sure you don't want to tell the complainants to email me their complaints or give them my office hours?"

Why was the mayor…Liv…so concerned? The scene in the auditorium? Something underpinning the whole thing, like McManus?

Make good decisions, Leo had said.

But Artur had no idea what good decisions were, except to be careful. And do his job.

As far as the potential scene waiting for him in the auditorium went? He'd faced worse. Heck; he'd *seen* worse. "Don't worry about it," he said, doing his best to convince her. "I'm fine. I'll be fine."

She looked at him and he'd swear he saw *something* in her eyes. Fear? Worry? Concern? He sure as heck didn't want to ask what was wrong, lest she consider it a personal affront or insult of some kind.

But he still couldn't stop thinking about it. Did she believe him? Was she worried about him?

"Are you sure?" she asked, clearly driven by either any of the protective emotions or business or politics or something. "I can go right in there and stop this right now."

There, the direction she pointed, was presumably the auditorium, and they would get nowhere if he didn't chop through this field of weedy concern before it turned into something else. "Listen to me," he said, crossing the distance between them but leaving space for her to push him away.

But she didn't; she stood still, looking up at him. "Listening."

He needed to tread carefully. "You can't fix things when you don't know what's broken. And if this is the only way where as many people who are here will really talk to us, to me, about what's bothering them? So be it."

"But…"

"If we do anything else," he continued, aware that he was on extremely shaky ground, "if we act as if we expect something to be wrong, then they'll think not only is something *actually* wrong, but also that we don't want to fix this. We're not on opposite sides, but if we come with sabers pointed in their direction, they'll think that we are."

Her nod popped a balloon of tension. "So," she said, folding her arms, as if she'd turned back into the savvy politician she'd been when he came into her office on Monday, "what's your plan then?"

That was easy.

"Act as if this is normal. Let them talk. Don't stop them. Let them cover me in tomatoes," he said, reminding her of what his position had been from the beginning. "Don't act as if complaining or poking holes in Flaire's awful plan isn't wanted."

He could see the moment where she heard Flaire's name and wondered what was going on. "But…I don't understand? Why does she have anything to do with this?"

"What they're upset about, at least, as far as I can tell, is Flaire's plan. That horrible plan is the reason why I got brought in here in the first place."

She nodded. "Okay. I get it. You can't create a foundation without knowing what's wrong."

"Exactly," he said, fully aware that she was pretty much repeating what he'd said; was this her way of digesting it? Either way he wasn't going to step in and cause her to second-guess herself. "Whatever happens next will work if the citizens of Briarwood buy in. And *only if they* buy in. That process begins tonight."

"Right. So, we do this." She wasn't tentative now. She was clear.

"Let's do this."

And then he followed her out of the room, waiting for her to show him where to sit.

Chapter Twelve

LIV TOOK A quick look at the clock as she stood in the hallway just outside the auditorium. The force of conviction in Artur's voice alone was enough to make her want to do things to him.

None of those things were appropriate to think about; all of them could derail her life before she got started.

Not everybody was Jerry McManus and yet Artur was…

Artur Rabinovitch was good at his job.

He was also smart enough to be able to bypass the wall of her concerns and force her to remember the thoughts she'd had before Burton Squires' email had arrived.

That? Made her weak in the knees.

No.

She was a professional woman, an elected official, prepared to leave one elected post for another. She couldn't be derailed by the way someone's sense of professional responsibility made her feel.

Resolute and clear, she signaled behind her and headed toward the stage. She didn't turn to see whether he was behind her; hearing his footsteps against the tile floor was enough.

After she walked through the curtain, she sat behind the table and podium that had been prepared for her and Artur's use. Microphones, pads, pens were all prepared.

On the front of the podium was the village seal. Reminding her what her purpose was.

Disciplined by a symbol, she shoved her feelings aside and turned her attention toward the documents in front of her. Everything was ready to go, and in usual Briarwood fashion, the list of people wanting to speak at this meeting had grown since she last saw it. Even flipping through the stapled pages was an exercise in anxiety.

But Artur sat next to her, ready for target practice. If he was ready to make something out of this, she needed to be as well.

"Hello and good evening, everyone," Liv began. "I want to thank you all for coming to tonight's special session. Mr. Artur Rabinovitch is here to listen to all of your concerns. All I ask is that you voice them in an orderly fashion as we call you to the microphone. I now turn the microphone over to him."

She watched him, doing her best to be mayoral or political or something professional, but failed miserably. The man looked too good in a suit, and wrapped as he was in the kind of conviction that appealed to her sense of justice made him impossible to resist.

"I want to thank Mayor Nachman and every single resident of Briarwood who came tonight and those who sent their concerns in by email or by petition," he said amidst the total silence in the auditorium. "I'm looking forward to listening to your concerns and then helping you create and build an event you can be proud of."

He paused, and she wondered as if he was allowing his words to sink in.

"Remember. Every single concern, no matter how small you think it may be, is welcome tonight. If something is important to you, it is important to the future of the event. We want a success, and an event won't succeed without your support."

"I want to make one quick note," Liv added after he stopped speaking. "I don't believe any direct questions need answers tonight amongst the comments we hear or have received."

The room started to rumble, but Liv was clear. "If there are questions that do arise, Mr. Rabinovitch can answer the questions that are within his purview, and at his discretion."

The rumbles continued and she turned toward Artur. The raised eyebrow was the only sign of his reaction; she didn't think she'd gone too far, but it was clear both he and the residents did.

"Comments are the priority," she said, attempting to clarify her own comments and defuse the tension that seemed to rise up around them. "Questions should come later but we'll talk about it if they come up. The goal of this meeting is to figure out what you think is wrong and what has gone wrong, so we can make an honest attempt at fixing what broke."

"More importantly," Artur said, as if he'd felt the break in the moment, "I want to make it clear that our interest is in creating something that will do Briarwood proud."

Do *Briarwood* proud.

His sense of justice was going to send her into sensory overdrive. Every single time he spoke about the event, he made it clear that it wasn't the team he was protecting or assisting.

It was the town.

Not only that, but he was making it clear that the town and its residents deserved better than what they'd been given. And that it was his job to help make sure they got better.

If nothing else, that was going to be her undoing, and before she could analyze his words yet again, she reminded herself she had a job to do.

"Now, let the meeting proceed."

And with a bang of her gavel, that's just what happened.

ARTUR DECIDED IT would be easier if he broke down the comments into categories, and halfway through the first part of the meeting, he'd gotten into a system.

The first few comments were concerns about lettering on

signs and spelling.

"I saw three dreidl graphics that had been placed on the PowerPoint," said one concerned resident, "and if this organization is sponsoring a dreidl sculpture for the town, I would be very concerned about how it's going to end up looking. Those graphics had the wrong letters on a few different sides, none of which could potentially be on a dreidl."

The next comments were about the proposed set of food items to be sold and served.

"Could you even have a Hanukkah festival without the traditional foods?" one resident wondered.

"Not even one drop of oil can be found anywhere in this proposed menu!" complained another. "It is SACRILEGE."

Three other people spoke specifically about some of the events planned. "We don't hunt gelt," said one annoyed man as he adjusted his glasses. "The only things we hunt are chametz before Passover and the afikomen during Passover. Where are the dreidls? Where are *our customs*?"

"Dreidls are probably spelled wrong," yelled one of the residents who'd complained about the lettering earlier in the meeting, "and confusing everybody."

Spelling was important, so were dreidls. He wrote a few notes and then let things continue.

"What bothers me," said the next resident, "is the disrespect on top of everything else. Not every Jew in Briarwood observes Shabbat the same way; heck some even go to the

congregation in Rivertown because it's got more Hebrew in
the service, and they read Torah on Friday nights, and others
go to Hollowville because they love the music and the choir.
Who knows why people go to different synagogues? But we
all respect the way the others observe. That does not include
staging an event that CONFLICTS with services ON THE
TEMPLE GROUNDS. That's not us. That's not Briarwood."

Artur nodded, remembered the idea he'd floated of a
stage set up by the sculpture in the center of town, and took
notes to see how he could make that happen.

But as the night went on, the temperature of the re-
sponders went up. More and more people were angry and
felt free to express that anger. Which was both a good and a
bad thing.

Good because they were comfortable and felt that their
anger could be both heard and understood. Bad? The fact
that they were this angry made him realize that nothing he
could have done would have prepared him for how badly
Flaire had messed everything up.

He also firmly believed that what saved him and kept
him here was his intention to let the population speak and
genuinely listen. With a generous assist from his lack of
desire to defend anything Flaire had done, his Judaism, and
his years in Rivertown. Without any of those, he'd be a
melted marshmallow on a smore of anger.

And yet there were still more comments coming.

Thankfully, he'd gotten inspired.

He scribbled a quick note, and passed it to the mayor. He felt like a little kid in school, passing notes to the teacher.

And yet it couldn't be helped.

She unfolded the paper and nodded.

"Ten-minute recess," Liv...Mayor Nachman said before banging the gavel authoritatively.

Which was exactly when he wanted. He nodded to the audience, stood, and followed Liv out of the room.

A RECESS.

What was going through his mind as he called for a recess?

Liv had absolutely no idea what was going on as they left the stage and walked into the backstage hallway; the man was a mystery. Which meant she had to actually *ask* the question. "You called for the break," she said as she stopped in front of the bank of lockers. "What's up?"

"Give me a second," he replied, throwing up his hand, palm out.

"Okay," she said.

He closed his eyes, as if he was gathering his thoughts.

Liv nodded, took a deep breath. Her anxiety, her concern wasn't meant to be his issue and she wasn't going to break the silence he clearly needed.

When he opened his eyes, the focus she saw almost scared her. "I think we're going to need a second meeting."

What?

Why?

But letting the thoughts run through and around her brain like mice in a maze wasn't going to do her any good. She had to use her words. "What's your reasoning here?"

"It's very obvious that the temperature of the meeting has gotten closer to boiling as we continued on," he began.

"Which means we need to stop. I don't want angry pitchforks."

"And," he said with a smile that melted her knees, "I've already decided I don't want to feel like the inside of a smore."

"So we're in agreement," she said as she prepared to head back through the door to the stage.

"No," he said, before she felt his fingers close around her wrist. "Wait…"

She stopped and turned as quickly as she could toward him. "Waiting. What's going on?"

"They're going to need to let this all out before they can give productive suggestions," he said. "And we've already told them we're looking for their suggestions."

"Okay…?"

He looked at her, as if he believed she'd lost her mind.

"What did you think this was going to be? Did you be-lieve me when I said I'd let myself be covered in lattes or tomatoes or anything?"

"I expected you'd deliver some kind of alternative plan. I mean you were talking already about the stage set up by the sculpture..."

He shook his head. "No," he said. "I mean yes I had ideas, and I'm continuing to have ideas. But I can't deliver an alternative project for a bunch of different reasons, the first of which is that you can't randomly come into a place and assume you know what the people want."

"You can't," she said, nodding her head before looking back up at him. "You're right. But then why a second meeting?"

"Let them talk today," he replied. "Then let them step away long enough to give us the constructive suggestions that we can use as a basis to create something that will make them happy."

"So, you're making them plan this event?"

He shook his head. "No. I'm asking their opinion as to what they want. Nobody's coming to a festival or event or exhibition where they have no part in it. They want hands and hearts and voices in it, not some random thing made by and for someone who is not them."

She nodded. "I like this," she said. "They'll let out some steam and then make suggestions, and then we'll use the suggestions to plan the event as best we can."

"Exactly," he said, and the breath she let out sounded like the end of a hot-air balloon.

"Okay then. We go back out there, let them finish the list, before setting a date for another meeting."

"Sounds good," he said. "I like this plan."

"Also," she said, deciding to push things a little. "You and I need to strategize and figure out things and the comments before we take any strategic steps."

"Before the next meeting," he asked, "or just as a postgame?"

"Postgame. I want to make sure you and I are on the same page."

He nodded. "Good thing. No strategic steps, no outside voices, until we've settled the game plan. When do you want to have this postgame?"

The words flew out of her mouth before she could think about their impact. "Tomorrow morning at Greenblatt's?"

The seconds she waited for his response extended way too long for her sake. But his answer was simple.

"Yes," he said. "I need breakfast knishes in my life."

"I'm glad to hear," she said, grinning. And as she walked back toward the meeting room, she took his hand in hers.

It felt as if they were ready to conquer anything.

Together.

Chapter Thirteen

A RTUR SQUEEZED LIV'S hand before they headed through the backstage area toward the podium, and let it go before they came into full sight.

But what kept him from thinking about how it felt to let her hand go was the complete lack of tension in the auditorium. It was as if someone had popped the atmosphere with a pin; everyone was calmer. Quieter. More relaxed.

Would they be more receptive to what was happening?

He didn't know, and yet more importantly, he couldn't figure out what had happened when they were gone. Did someone talk to the residents?

He wasn't sure; as he started to settle down behind the table, Paul Levitan caught his eye and gave him a *look*.

Hmmmm.

What did this mean?

He met the mayor's expression, only to see she was shrugging, or pointing back at the paper. Did she catch the look on Paul Levitan's face?

"Make good choices," Leo had said as he was leaving Abe's.

For not the first time that night he found himself returning to that statement, trying to figure out what the heck his friend meant.

But as he couldn't figure it out, he organized his papers and did his best to settle back into the process of listening and taking notes until the meeting was over. When that happened and Liv banged her gavel, he walked with her to the parking lot.

"What do you think happened while we were in recess?" he asked.

"I have no idea," she said. "None at all. And I have no idea what Paul Levitan did. He and the rest of the chamber have a mind of their own, I think."

Which meant what? Had he walked into some kind of local conspiracy come to life? Did she know about what happened with McManus's Pub?

"Anyway," she said, "I guess we'll find out."

"Probably at the worst possible time," he managed, his brain still whirring in an attempt to pull something out of this night, aside from the notes he'd put together.

"Probably," she said with a smile. "See you tomorrow?"

"Breakfast knishes."

"Yes," she said, smiling.

"Looking forward to it," he said. And knowing a dismissal when he heard it, he headed back to Abe's.

Except he couldn't get to sleep, having tried and failed to slow down his brain.

Luckily for him, he had notes to make presentable for his

meeting with Liv. Questions and thoughts and…

An email.

He put his papers down next to his laptop before switching into his email.

An invitation.

To a lunch with selected members from the chamber of commerce. At Levitan's.

The next day.

He checked the other emails included on the distribution list and saw the Mayor's.

Which meant this was not in invitation but a summons. And there was no other response than yes.

Which he gave, cc'ing Liv.

As he typed the email, things fell into place. Levitan or someone from the chamber had been responsible for quieting the room. And he'd bet he'd find out what the cost was at this meeting.

What did he want? What did they want?

Did this have anything to do with McManus?

He had absolutely no idea, and even more importantly, he didn't have time to ponder about it beyond sending his agreement to attend the luncheon, because just as he sent it, a separate email from the mayor came in. He read through it, and the important part read:

Change of location. Meet me in my office. I'll have breakfast waiting. We'll prepare. And strategize.

And coffee, he replied. *I don't think I'm going to sleep.*

You should at least try, came another email from the

mayor. *It's going to be a long one.*

I have notes, he returned. *Gotta prep for the meeting with you and then the lunch.*

You have Shabbat plans?

She'd switched to the email program's adjacent chat app, and he wondered why she asked. But he answered anyway. *Best friend and a few others in Rivertown. You?*

Family, but I'm not going to sleep either. Email me the notes when you're done?

Sounds good.

He took a long swallow of the glass of water, before settling in for a long night.

Knowing that Liv would be on the other end kept him awake for reasons other than why he was in town.

LIV HAD MADE the mistake of waiting for the notes and then reading through them instead of going to sleep.

I like this, she'd messaged Artur after going through the notes.

Thank you. You think this is what they're going to be talking about?

I don't know. Racking my brain. Maybe I'll have answers in a few hours.

See you then?

If she was bolder, braver, she'd tell him to come now, when she was staring at her crystal cabinet, sitting under a blanket on the couch and holding her phone.

Instead, she typed, *See you then.*

And tried not to think too much about what it would feel like to have him there with her, in the cozy night, in her town house, sitting next to her on the couch, his warmth keeping her warm, his voice calming her...

Instead, she forced herself to think about the chamber of commerce's motives.

What did the chamber want? What was their concern?

She needed to figure out their agenda before the meeting. God forbid it was their attempt to act like a governmental chaperone.

Literally. Not figuratively.

The very last thing she needed was to be confronted with the business owners of Briarwood reminding her that her reputation was their reputation and that both needed to be clean.

In front of Artur. Who stirred feelings in her, a man who made her wish for a second she didn't have to lock the doors of her personal life, and hide away in front of anybody and everybody who may have known who she was. Someone who was in Briarwood to fix the mess that had been made of a gift she wanted to give the town.

So instead of an invitation to her place where she could give him something personal, the next morning she brought him sour cream...to go along with bagels and coffee and other associated spreads.

For professional reasons.

And resisted the urge to call and check on him, simply got dressed, organized and headed into the office to prep for the meeting.

When he arrived, she could barely keep her jaw off the desk. "Take it easy," she said half to him and half to herself, as he came in the room. "Let's have coffee; you can have sour cream; we'll have bagels and spreads and then we'll hash it out."

"Already with the calming?"

She smiled, gesturing to the spread. "Can't help it apparently. Providing breakfast turns me into, well, someone who hovers."

"You got me sour cream," he said. "That is enough, more than enough."

The look on his face, slightly lost, slightly excited was enough to knock her over. "People don't remember? Don't indulge you?"

"My friends get it," he admitted. "Way too many people think it's weird."

"Where did it…" she began before deciding it was probably a bad idea to ask him this here, now. "Never mind."

"Memories," he said, answering the question she didn't want to ask. "It's always been comforting. Grandmother's cooking, and when we moved to Rivertown, it wasn't weird to ask for it. I kept asking."

She nodded, taking her coffee into her hands. "I get it," she said. Because she did. "My sister could always find pickles in the fridge growing up, and she made sure they were in the fridge wherever she went. It made me feel better to make sure she had them."

Around the bagel he'd covered in cream cheese, he nodded. "You're a good sister."

"Sometimes," she said with a laugh. "Siblings are hard. Do you have any?"

"Friends," he said. "Friends that act like siblings."

She nodded. "Rivertown, Shabbas?"

"That's the one," he said. "Friend I was with at Levitan's when we bumped into each other. Another knows the guy at the Pasta Station."

Connections to local businesses…

And the chamber of commerce.

"I wonder," she said, beginning to voice her concern. "If that has something to do with the meeting and the agenda. Connections that have the chamber of commerce wondering about connections and crossing and interests."

He nodded. "And where mine lie?"

"Wait," she managed, the thoughts running through her head as she tried to corral the words and understand what he was saying. "What happened?"

He put his coffee down on her desk and looked up at her; she tried not to faint. "What do you mean what happened?"

"I mean," she began, trying not to sigh, "what happened to make you think they're concerned about where your interests lie?"

"Aaaaah," he said. "Right. So. My friend was yelling at the guy from the Pasta Station when he introduced me. He…Maricelli, I think his name is?"

She could picture Frank Maricelli yelling at someone on the sidewalk. He wasn't a bad guy, but he was protective. "Yeah. That's him."

"The reason why there was yelling, was that Maricelli had seen…us with my jacket when we were outside."

And they must have seen something at the meeting, which made her realize that she'd been right. The chamber was, in fact, acting like a governmental chaperone.

Great.

But just to make sure, she continued the conversation. "Why was your friend yelling at Maricelli?"

Was he blushing? Was there color suddenly on his cheeks. "Maricelli was accusing me of behavior unbecoming," he managed. "Leo, my friend, was taking exception to it."

"Leo…?"

"Fratelli," he replied. "I've known him since I moved to Rivertown."

Better and better, she thought to herself.

Not. "I think the chamber is going to test you and me about what your actual purpose is being here," she finally said.

"Right," he said. "We have our postgame as part of the

meeting? Set the agenda with them?"

"Or at least," she said, "send your notes to the chamber, let them know that we're going to be discussing the agenda you put together."

"I'll be prepared," he said.

And if she hadn't lost her mind already, she was a goner.

Chapter Fourteen

WALKING INTO LEVITAN'S with Liv…Mayor Nachman was completely different than walking into Levitan's with Abe. Or even different from the time he'd come in looking for advice and information.

This was business. He wasn't on the job searching for help or an ally; this was the job.

Having Liv with him was another story, and he already knew he was on shaky ground.

Somewhat shaky ground.

Making complex a situation that he wished was very easy. Of course the first time there were feelings like what he was feeling, he was in the middle of a job he couldn't mess up.

"Mayor, Mr. Rabinovitch?"

Paul Levitan looked different, nervous as he stood in front of them.

"Yes," Artur said.

"This way," he said, leading the way toward the back of the restaurant area he'd been in with Abe.

But instead of going into the kitchen area, Levitan

turned and led them past bathrooms to an office.

Jennifer Cohen, Carol and a few others were waiting. "Please sit down," Levitan said as he closed the door.

"Thank you for coming," Levitan continued as Artur settled into a chair next to the mayor. "We're concerned about the state of the Hanukkah celebration and a few other items."

"I informed the group that based on information I had and that they should have, I was not concerned," Jennifer Cohen said.

"But a few of us volunteered to serve on a special committee," Levitan continued. "To act as liaisons between the larger committee and the both of you, to ensure things were on the up and up after…last night's meeting."

Carol added, "It was a conversation that lasted late into the night, and some of the other members needed to be put into their places."

Artur had three guesses, and he didn't think he'd actually need more than one.

"But the bottom line," Levitan continued, "was that we insisted on our assistance, in helping this event to be fruitful."

Insisted, huh.

Levitan went on. "Let's start from the beginning. Do either of you think there's anything salvageable about what came out of last night's meeting?"

Whichever of the two of them had the idea to go

through the notes he'd taken the night before, print them, and put them in binders was a genius.

"Yes," Liv said, taking out the binders from the tote bag she carried. "Here. Take one, and we'll give you a few minutes to go over them before addressing the situation."

"We discussed the meeting," Artur added. "And organized the comments before coming up with basic ways to address each of the issues that came up."

Levitan nodded, and Artur turned to Liv. He wasn't sure how to translate the look on her face, but it looked good. He wanted to say something, but the sound of the pages being flipped was too crucial.

"Absolutely," Carol said. "Graphics need to be triple-checked, to fix all the concerns about spelling. For sure."

Jennifer Cohen added with a smile, "And the food traditions need to be taken into account. Gluten-free and parve items need to be on the list as well as fried foods. They need to be added where everybody can enjoy them."

Of course it was Jenifer Cohen who noticed the food.

"I think we can take care of some of that for sure." Levitan added. "But didn't Rivertown have some innovative ideas about food?"

Artur nodded. "Yes," he said, but knowing his audience consisted of a few people who had connections to Hollowville, he smiled. "But Hollowville did it first. Not exactly in the same way as Rivertown, but the food hall at the Hollowville Festival is a good example of how to involve the community in creating a food space that meshes tradition and innovation."

"I wonder," said Carol, her expression thoughtful. Of course Artur had a feeling of where she was going. "I might be able to get some help there. You too, Paul."

And knowing Carol the way he did, he was entirely unsurprised at Paul Levitan's reaction. "Absolutely."

"But, what really stands out to me is this idea of a staging area." Jennifer Cohen said, "It takes the events away from temple grounds and allows events to be held in a way that wouldn't disturb services. I wonder…"

"What are you thinking, Jennifer?" Mayor Liv asked.

"I wonder what the rabbi would think about moving *Tot Shabbat* to the staging area, or have a service *in front* of the dreidl, depending on how cold it gets…"

"Or even a Havdalah singalong," murmured Artur. "Or something like that."

"Oh, that would be fun," Liv managed alongside the excited murmurs.

That smile was going to be the death of him. "And that would be a beautiful meld of traditions and community."

"Exactly," the mayor said, smiling again. "Speaking of melding traditions, I wonder if your idea of turning the chess table setup into a dreidl table would be a good one to add."

"I can see it," Paul Levitan said.

"Yep," Jennifer Cohen replied. "I really like that."

"Good thoughts," Carol said. "I have someone on staff

who may be able to help. And by on staff, I mean my second in command here and in Hollowville."

Yep. The light laughter and a grin in his direction. Carol knew what she was doing.

"I also think you should probably talk to the head of the JHPA, involve him.," Jennifer Cohen interjected.

The laughter continued, and he could see the blush in Liv's cheeks.

Hmmmm...

"He's absolutely willing to take part, so once there's a role for him to play, I'll involve him" she said.

"Good enough."

And as the meeting came to a close, he found himself feeling slightly better and yet slightly worse. Even more uncertain about his standing with Liv.

AFTER THEY FINISHED the meeting, they headed back to her office. He was gathering his things rather quickly and she suddenly looked up at him.

"What?"

"I wondered, well you look like you're in a rush. Do you have somewhere to be?"

"Eventually, just like you," he replied, that smile again. "Why?"

She sighed. "I don't know what to make of that meeting."

He shrugged and the rise and fall of his shoulders made her smile. "I think that we're in a good place. It's a friendly crowd, stepping in to separate us from the rest of the chamber. Don't think it's anything to worry about."

She nodded, though she wasn't sure what to believe. "You know the person who organized the festival in Hollowville?"

"Yes. Friend of a friend. And you know the head of the JHPA."

"He's marrying my cousin," she said. "Which, yes. I realize. The Rivertown friends?"

"Yes. My best friend's wife, also a friend from high school, lived in Hollowville for a few years, and one of her close friends works with Carol."

"The web we weave," she said with a laugh. "So many connections."

"Strings and threads," he said. "Do you want to start massaging those connections before next week's meeting? Maybe next weekend? I might be able to convince my best friend to barbecue. In his backyard."

"Backyard in Rivertown?"

"Yep. Kosher barbecue." He paused, and she wasn't sure. "Although if you want to stay in Briarwood, I have another friend who might be interested in throwing a select party."

"So, my choices are a select party in Briarwood or a pop-up kosher barbecue for a select number of people. In Rivertown."

"Yes," he said, grinning. "Anyway, you want to come? Be one of those select people? Massage connections?"

Since the disastrous mayoral re-election where Jerry McManus made her secrets public, she'd made so many choices: to hide away, to spend time with a tiny group of her relatives if she wasn't campaigning or working. Nothing else.

She'd hidden her heart away.

She'd hidden her life away.

It had given her political success, and she enjoyed her career.

And it had turned the chamber of commerce into watch-dogs.

The very last thing she needed was someone else trying to upset her carefully organized life.

Except she needed to admit she already had. And the fact that she was even thinking about saying yes, well... But she needed to clarify. "Are you asking me out, Mr. Rab-inovitch?"

"Depends," he said.

"On what?"

"On if you're ready to explore what's going on between us," he said. "But if all you're ready for is business, and massaging contacts, that's fine too."

"Do you want a business meeting, or do you want a date?" And that was a question she didn't realize she was going to ask until she actually did. "I mean..."

"It's fine," he said. And then he paused, looking up at her, making her heart stop. "Are you ready to jump off the cliff with me, or are you in the mood to simply drive to the parking lot?"

She laughed, and it wasn't a bad thing. It was...good. It was nice. He definitely was going to be the death of her. "Can I put a hold on the decision?"

He nodded. "Just let me know as soon as you can."

"Will do," she said. "Though I will say if I was going to agree to something, the idea of a kosher backyard barbecue in Rivertown would be a better choice."

"I'll keep that in mind," he continued as if he'd caught the thoughts running through her head. "I'll keep everyone on a need-to-know basis."

"I appreciate it," she said. And then all she could do was watch as he finished packing up his stuff before he headed out the door.

She had things to do and choices to make.

Quickly.

Chapter Fifteen

S HABBAT DINNER WITH Abe and Batya was supposed to be a welcome distraction from the barrage of thoughts running through his head. Except he had to go and ask Liv if she wanted to 'explore what was going on between them' at a barbecue party that didn't exist.

Yet.

Because he had to convince Abe to host it.

"What's up?"

He blinked, looked up at Batya as she brought the brisket to the table. "I don't know what you mean."

"You were supposed to update me on the meeting," she said. "And you've been making ridiculous noises all night. What's up?"

Aah, right. He hadn't spoken to Batya because he'd pulled an all-nighter and then ran off to Liv's office to debrief before dealing with the pretzel of that meeting in Levitan's.

"Come on," Abe said, that undeniable expression on his face. "I made matzah balls, so you need to talk."

Sacred reminders of their long-term friendship. He was,

in fact doomed. Which meant he needed to spill. "I need help," he said, getting to the point of the matter, "I might need you to create something."

Abe raised an eyebrow and looked at Batya before turning back to him. "This is the most coherent you've been in a long time. Usually you beat around six bushes and expect me to dig under bush number seven for a surprise."

"Sorry," he managed. "I'm in a pickle."

Abe raised an eyebrow. "Dill? Kosher? Bread and butter?"

"Kosher. Definitely kosher." He swallowed. "Two of them."

"Two of them, huh?" Batya asked as she brought the challah to the table. "Let's make motzi over this beautiful loaf, and then you tell the story over dinner because I want to hear it."

And so they said the blessings: first over the candles on the counter, then over the bread.

"Now," said Abe as he passed the challah around. "Tell the story and then we'll talk more."

Artur proceeded to tell the story of what happened; about Liv, about working with her, the weird actions by the chamber of commerce and Leo...and his fascination with her despite all of that.

"Let me get this straight," Abe said with a grin, and paused for dramatic effect.

Artur nodded, knowing he was in trouble.

"You need me to pull together a barbecue party."

"Yes," he said. "Maybe a way to, you know, try your recipes for new places and meet some people."

Abe laughed; his best friend could see right through him. Hopefully the prospect of all of this was enough to make it happen.

"Right. And if I agree to do this thing…a random popup that's accessible to you and a small group of people, I'll be covering up the fact you're asking this woman…the Mayor of Briarwood no less, on a date."

Artur nodded. "Yes," he said, realizing how ridiculous he was being. "That's what I'm asking you."

Abe didn't respond immediately, which Artur would chalk up to his good luck, the timing, or whatever plan his best friend was forming in his head.

"So," Abe finally said, breaking the silence and making Artur a little nervous. "What's the catch? For me, I mean. What do I get out of it?"

"Yes," Batya said; she'd been strangely silent, which was unlike her. He'd known her a long time, not as long as he'd known Abe, but long enough to know this was out of character for her and did not bode well. "I mean I certainly see the benefits for you, Artur, but what does my husband get for doing this?"

He had to think fast.

What could he give Abe and Batya that they'd accept? What could he do to justify this ridiculous favor?

And then he got it.

The one thing neither of them could say no to.

"How about this," he said. Hoping this gamble would work. "You can invite a select number of people who will spend the time giving me the business? Me specially, and not her because this is…"

"A cover-up," Abe replied. "Yes. I get it. You're going to get the business of course, but from a select group of people of my choosing, who will meet her and *behave*, before giving you the business later?"

He nodded. "Yes."

"Is that the offer on the table?"

Artur nodded. "Yes."

"And when would you want me to do this?"

"Next weekend? I'm not that horrible a person."

"You're not horrible but you're not as altruistic as you think." Abe turned to Batya as Artur waited. "What do you think?"

Batya took another slice of the brisket. "I think we might be able to pull this off. A fun barbecue party before I take off for a bit and you get deep into work?"

"A fun pop-up thing." Abe nodded his head and Artur realized this was going to happen. Which surprised him, but also relieved him.

"I like this," Abe continued before turning to Batya. "Who do we ask?"

"Leo, Sapna, Claire and her girlfriend…"

"Whose name we don't yet know," Artur pointed out, as

they fell into conversation about their old High School Quiz Bowl teammate.

"Claire isn't sure whether this is serious," Batya interjected. "So she's waiting. It's like a meeting-the-parents vibe. Speaking of she's...do you think the mayor will want to bring people?"

"She's got two cousins and a sister," Artur replied. "So possibly three, six, somewhere in between."

"That works," Batya said. "But also, Sarah and Isaac, Anna and Jacob."

"Any permutation of those," Artur replied. "And Sarah might be a draw."

Abe raised an eyebrow. "Why?"

Batya shook her head. "Were you not listening when he was talking about how it seems he needs a Hanukkah festival consultant, but don't call it a festival because Briarwood is full of snobs. And we're in Rivertown so we can say that."

Artur wasn't sure which line he liked better. "And this is why I adore you."

"I thought it was the challah."

"My brisket, her challah and my matzah ball soup. Anyway, back to business."

"Yes?"

"Party. Pop-up. Invite her. Introduce her."

Difficult questions answered on a Friday night. All he had to do now was wait for Liv to give him a response.

LIV BARELY MADE it through Shabbat dinner before her sister dragged her outside to her parents' back deck.

It was still a beautiful view, even with the chill setting in, and a glass of wine that her sister made her bring.

"Now," Naomi said. "What's going on with you? Exactly."

"I'm debating a really bad decision."

"Are there any good choices these days?" Naomi asked, shaking her head. "And this is you, so it can't really be that horrible."

"It's worse than you think."

"Does it involve bailing a bolted bride's mother out of jail after she assaulted the groom's mother and half the wedding party for daring to insinuate the bride eloped with her girlfriend? Even after she sent wedding photos to her very happy former fiancé from Las Vegas?"

Liv blinked. "That is…"

"Tell me about it," said Naomi as she turned on the fire pit. "Never have I seen a woman in such denial. So, is it worse than that kind of nonsense?"

"No," she admitted. "It's not."

Liv met her cousin's eyes, and the inspection there. The searching for a particular problem was going to drive her nutty. "Is it something that would make you…step outside the cage you've put yourself in?"

"It's not about a cage," she said. "I mean the last time I admitted to a personal life, it got used against me in ways that *still* have repercussions. I don't know how to act; I can't trust my instincts and I don't want people close to me to get hurt."

"People close to you, as in who? Your family who loves you? Who?"

"Naomi," she said with a long, extended sigh. "Can you not make me inventory the people in my life who I think might get hurt by my choices and instead help me... I don't know, try to deal with the fact that it's okay to choose?"

"Yourself? Your right to feel something? Your right to add people into your life? What? Or rationalize why it's better to keep people out, because if you didn't want to let someone in, we wouldn't be having this conversation. Am I right?"

Liv didn't answer, and Naomi nodded.

"Right. So how did this start, and yes I remember hearing about that one Shabbat where Flaire and asked if she could take the space from the rabbi's sermon to introduce herself to the congregation, which was probably the beginning of the end for Flaire, which led to that horrible proposal, and the reason this guy is there."

Liv told Naomi the story, ending with: "So yes. I wish I wasn't completely affected by the way he's taken this whole thing on his shoulders. He's not only brandishing a sword but he's falling on one. He shouldn't have to."

"You know," Naomi said with a laugh, "if I were someone else, I'd ask you where this Liv was when Judith was talking about the importance of people's love lives."

"Don't remind me," she said. "Besides. I'm not actually making bad decisions yet, just debating this."

"I want to know who *was* manifesting the treat and the bad decisions then," Naomi said. "Because you're rarely, if ever, on the verge of making choices that you're concerned will make people remember you have a personal life outside of politics."

"All of this is the prelude to the decision."

"Okay," Naomi said. "So, you're on the verge of making what you think is a bad decision, which is most likely related to a relationship that may or may not be professional and something you might potentially want to make personal. Am I right?"

Liv nodded, trapped into a conversation that was getting deeper and deeper by the second. "Yes," she said. "You are."

"And what bad decision is the problem here?"

"He's invited me to a barbecue pop-up at his friend's house in Rivertown."

Naomi blinked. "I did not ever expect to hear words like that coming out of your mouth, but also I barely expect to hear those words strung together." She paused for a second. "Guy's from Rivertown?"

"Yes?"

"Friends with Judith's boss?"

"I don't know the guy, and I don't know Judith's boss. All I know is that his best friend is the barbecue guy who's going to open a restaurant and he's testing recipes and he, the fixer, invited me to the pop-up."

"Sounds familiar," Naomi continued, in that irritating way her sister had of connecting things that were entirely too disparate. "Kosher barbecue?"

Liv nodded. "Yes. Again, he, the fixer…"

"If you're going to call the guy anything, you should use his name. What is the guy's name by the way?"

"Artur," Liv said. "Don't know the friend's name but the fixer is Artur…"

"Who is, in fact, the fixer Leah's looking at for her client, and knows Judith's boss. Which meant his friend catered Ash and Judith's b'nai mitzvah party but can't do their wedding."

"Who did you go with for the wedding, by the way?" Liv wondered, trying to get her brain off of the web of connections she'd walked into.

"Someone who my boss has used before. Kosher et cetera, et cetera. They're paying through the roof for this, but it's good I guess."

Liv nodded. "Got it."

"So, are you going to the pop-up or is that the decision you think is the bad one?"

She could tell her sister even if she couldn't admit it to anybody else. "I want to," she said. "I really want to. But it's a horrible decision."

"Livvy," Naomi said, putting down her wineglass and crossing over to where she sat.

Naomi's embraces were wonderful, and Liv let herself be swept up into her sister's arms. "Livvy," Naomi said again. "It's dinner. It's not the downfall of your political career. Who knows."

But it never was just dinner. Nobody ever invited someone to 'dinner' without strings. Ever. She separated herself from her sister and sighed. "The chamber of commerce is watching me, and him. They called us to Levitan's to make sure we were making *professional* progress after the meeting yesterday. If I go, and someone sees me…"

"This is a pop-up by someone who just finished creating the barbecue recipes used at Levitan's. Isn't he someone who could possibly be convinced to open something more permanent in Briarwood? If nothing else, think of it as a business expedition," her sister said, her eyes flashing.

"It's complicated," Liv said, knowing she really didn't want to be. "It's always complicated."

"Life is complicated, as is love," Naomi replied. "And don't even think about it."

But despite her sister's warning, she did in fact travel down the ridiculous rabbit hole that had been the disaster of her love life: guys who almost derailed her career before it started, guys who thought it was a horrible idea for someone her age to run for office, others who asked her out only to pitch her an event in the middle of a fancy restaurant. Not to mention the man who turned the chamber of commerce into her own personal watchdog.

But all she said was, "Just because not everybody is McManus, doesn't mean my life or my instincts aren't affected by it. I don't need this event to destroy both my life and career, Mimi."

"You're using the nickname," Naomi said. "That means business, so business I shall give. This is dinner. This is a very carefully planned invitation to eat food you already like. Worst comes to worst, you eat the food and don't discuss it again."

Only hours later did she realize she hadn't taken the opportunity to quiz Naomi on her own love life, or even admit that she'd decided to say yes.

That is, if Artur remembered to ask her again. If she had to bring it up, it was fate. Because the bottom line was that she couldn't initiate anything. Too much was on the line for her to remind him if he hadn't had the intention to begin with.

Chapter Sixteen

DESPITE ALL OF Artur's concerns about what had happened at the initial meeting with the subsection of the chamber of commerce, it turned out that with a few exceptions it had, in fact, been a prelude to suggestions delivered by some of the chamber members during the second meeting itself.

"Story time involving the temple youth group, with a special group of selections from Briarwood Tales celebrating Jewish authors and Hanukkah stories." The suggestion came from Jennifer Cohen and Carol.

"Some of the Briarwood restaurant owners and food vendors have volunteered to create Hanukkah-appropriate menus based on the cuisine of their menus," said Peter Levitan. "There is a great deal of Hanukkah food from all over the world, and a great deal of it can be represented in Briarwood."

"There are a few conversations that need to take place," said the superintendent of schools, "but I think the district and the boosters would love to organize an outdoor sports section."

The list of suggestions continued on, and the inspiration was a red sports car, flying through the autobahn of his mind. Visions and photos popped up like random gas stations. This was absolutely wonderful.

They weren't out of the woods yet, but it felt really good.

"There are so many wonderful ideas," said Liv, full mayor persona on display. "It's going to be difficult to narrow them down. Thank you all."

As she banged the gavel and the meeting ended, he found his head spinning.

"Walk me to the car?"

He nodded. "Absolutely," he said.

They said their goodbyes and as they left the building, side by side, they headed toward her car.

"You're quiet," she said in the glow of the streetlights by town hall. "What's going on?"

He had to be careful on how he couched this from the beginning, knowing both the mayor and Briarwood wanted an event of their own, that wasn't like any of the other Hudson Valley Hanukkah events, not even in name.

"I wonder," he said after pausing for just a little, "what the feasibility is of having a *multi-day event cycle?*"

"What?" she asked. "Explain."

She looked intrigued, which was a victory. "Well, how about you make the *arrival of the dreidl sculpture* the core of a series of events that take place over a few days? Center the whole thing around it, like you see with the arrival of an honored guest—human or horticultural—that happens during this time of year."

She snorted.

Maybe he went a little too far. Hmm.

She interjected, "I like this idea."

"I'm sensing a 'but'?"

She nodded. "We have to be very, very, very careful."

"Aah yes. It's a multi-day cycle celebrating the arrival of Hanukkah and the Briarwood dreidl sculpture."

"Great idea," she said with a grin. "As long as nobody starts singing *here comes the dreidl, made out of clay, spinning and bringing joy every day...*"

He laughed as a vision of a dreidl wrapped in a white ribbon spun through his brain. Of course, her song cued up another musical memory of his. But his voice was worse than hers, so he didn't even try to sing it; a reference was going to be better. "Just don't make a dreidl lane. That would make it worse."

"As long as the rabbi, the cantor, and the youth group aren't spinning the dreidl down that absolutely not renamed street, we'll be fine," the mayor replied.

He could see the joy in her eyes under the lights; his guess was that she was desperately trying to hold back a tidal wave of laughter.

She was gorgeous.

Which meant he had to shove things back on track. "Dreidl as signifier of Shabbat?"

Liv grinned. "Menorah Havdalah."

This kind of banter was yet another reason why he enjoyed spending time with her.

H wanted to spend more, which brought him back to the butterfly of a topic flittering around them. He'd asked her a question and though he didn't want to push, he needed to let Abe know her answer, good or bad, yes or no. Theoretically it didn't matter what answer he was going to give Abe, but the bottom line was that it did.

To him.

He wanted her to come but...

"You here?"

"Yeah. Sorry. Mind went elsewhere."

"Would you mind telling me where it went—if it's not too private?"

He could take the easy way out, but he'd never been that kind of person. "My friend Abe," he said. "I need to tell him *something*, whatever it is."

"I'll go," she said, looking around, as if to see if they were alone for sure. "But don't make a big deal about this. I just...want to be. You know?"

He did. "I won't even make a big deal to myself when I think about it," he said. "I'll just tell Abe to take it calm. Sound good?"

She nodded. "Yes."

"Saturday night, okay?"

"Yes. Can you arrange the meeting with the Hanukkah

consultant Carol was talking about?"

Whiplash. But it was the best kind. "How about tomorrow?" he asked.

"Sounds good," she said. "I'll make sure we have something lined up with the JHPA president in the next few days following."

And her smile? It lit everything up. Not just her face but the world.

And he couldn't stop himself from falling into this wild, wonderful feeling.

Which was going to be trouble. So much trouble.

The best kind of trouble.

THE NEXT MORNING, Liv shook off the stardust and headed toward Briarwood Tales; that was what his message had said, after all.

Meet me at 9 a.m. at Briarwood Tales; we'll meet our Hanukkah consultant there.

There was a good space in the parking lot, and there was a chill in the air.

It was gorgeous.

She was going to miss days like this, she reflected as she headed into the store. It was one of her favorite places, and from what she knew, the Hanukkah consultant was the assistant manager.

She wondered if he'd made it;, if he found a parking

space.

Her fears dissipated, because when she looked up, he was already there, chatting away with the dark-curly-haired woman—who had been introduced to her once as the co-owner.

"Hello?"

"Mayor Nachman," the woman said with a smile. "Good to see you this morning. Glad this is my in-store day here in Briarwood."

Livvy raised an eyebrow. "Nice to see you too. Um…"

"Oh I'm sorry," the woman said, shaking her head. "I need to introduce myself. I'm Sarah Goldman-Lieberman."

"Nice to officially meet you," she said, trying to think of why that name sounded so familiar.

"Hi." Artur.

And with one word, all of Livvy's thoughts went out the window. "Hi," she managed.

"Sarah is going to help us," he said. "She's…"

And that's when the lightning bolt went off above Livvy's head. Sarah Goldman-Lieberman was the woman in charge of the Hollowville Hanukkah Festival, having started in that position the year it went big and made Hanukkah into part of the tourism calendar the way Halloween was.

"Yes!" Liv said. "You planned the famous Hollowville Festival."

"I did," Sarah said; the pride in the other woman's eyes made Liv even more grateful for what was happening.

And to Artur for connecting them.

"I'm just glad that though Hollowville was the first," Sarah continued. "There are so many others popping up. I think it's important for municipalities to recognize the religious diversity of their residents, and plan accordingly."

"She's being modest," Artur added, like he needed to fact-check this woman. "But she was also called in as a consultant in Rivertown. And I suspect that her fingers have been involved in a bunch of other festivals."

"Which is why I really appreciate the fact that you're willing to spend time here, in Briarwood, helping us figure out what our event is going to look like," Liv added, even more excited about the prospect of what was going to happen.

"Do you have a name for it yet? A direction?" Sarah asked.

Liv nodded. "It's going to be organized around the sculpture, so we're going to be treating it more like the opening of an art exhibit as opposed to a festival."

Sarah nodded, and as they sat down she pulled out a notebook and a bright blue pen with a menorah on the top. "Well, you're right," the consultant said as she opened the notebook. "Hollowville is a festival, but its central event is the menorah lighting, and the menorah itself."

"Right," Liv replied. "But our sculpture is going to be a dreidl."

"Which seems to be a less active part of the event," the

consultant confirmed, making more notes, which made the menorah bend with the movement. "So more like Rivertown, which is a central event that takes place over a few days, that starts with a class for the participants. First year there were kinks that had to be ironed out, but things went really well and have been for the past few years."

"It's the talk of the town," Artur said. "I mean Rivertown."

Rivertown was Artur's hometown after all; she needed to ask him more about it. But that would be later. "I figured," she said.

"So, what's your sense of Briarwood?" Sarah asked. "Because I think we're getting somewhere."

"Briarwood's...opening," Liv said, feeling more comfortable with the wording the more she spoke, "is going to be centered around the delivery of the sculpture. But because the sculpture doesn't so much play an active part in the celebration of the holiday, I see the space we're creating as more of a gathering spot."

"There are options for the spot where we celebrate," Artur added; this confusing, perplexing, amazing man who got joy from planning this event with her.

"I love this," Sarah added. "You always have the best ideas," she said, turning toward Artur.

Their banter reminded her of the way she talked to Judith or Naomi. And it was wonderful. And if pressed, Liv would think that Sarah was also part of his extended friends circle, the ones he liked to spend time with during Hanukkah. And if she had to bet anything, she'd bet Sarah was one of the people who liked large Hanukkah celebrations.

But she didn't say that.

Instead, her ridiculous brain pointed out the fact that this woman knew Artur enough to know his business. Thankfully, the rational side reminded her that it was Artur's business to have all sorts of connections and know all sorts of people so that he knew who to call on when he needed someone to fix a problem.

She wondered if long after this event was over, she'd be able to be one of his experts. Local-Governments-R-Us, call Liv Nachman at 914-222-2222, or some random number that was easy to dial, for assistance in completing town business.

"Are there events that have been suggested?" Sarah asked, bringing Liv's attention back to the conversation. "Have you looked at feasibility?"

"I think we're looking at a multi-day event cycle," Artur said, "What I think we need from you at this stage is maybe an understanding of what the days might look like."

"How many feasible event slots," Liv clarified. "And then I think we can narrow down the events based on the slots."

"Do you have priorities?" Sarah asked, clearly focusing on the event. Unlike Liv, who was sneaking glances at Artur. "Do you want competing events, or do you want the town solely focused on one event at a time?"

Liv tapped her fingers on the table before looking back up at Sarah. "Let's figure out two different event schedules, one on each side."

Sarah nodded, and took the papers Liv passed over, the list of events and spaces as well as timing. "Give me a few minutes," Sarah said with a smile. "I'll take a look."

And as they stepped away from the table, Artur looked up at her before turning back to Sarah. "Do you want us to grab lunch?"

She couldn't help but smile...even as her stomach chimed in and added its opinion.

"Oh, that would be lovely," Sarah said. "Get whatever. I mean, if you meant to include me."

"I'll take that as a yes. And," Artur continued, "of course I mean to include you. Liv, do you want to come with me?"

She nodded, grinned back at him. "Sounds good."

And after a quick second of conversation where Artur confirmed Sarah's number and food tastes, she followed him outside.

"How do you know her again?"

He nodded, and the smile made his face as bright as the sun. "Her best friend is my best friend's wife, and her husband is part of an art crew in Brooklyn that includes a sofer."

She blinked. "There's an art crew in Brooklyn who knows a sofer?"

He laughed. "You'd think they'd be in style."

Now it was her turn to laugh. "But that means her husband knows my cousin's boyfriend."

"Your cousin...?"

"Leah," she replied, remembering that he didn't know the ins and outs of her family. Which meant she had to be specific and clarify. "Leah's boyfriend is a sofer in Brooklyn."

"Does he trade under the name 'the hot sofer'?"

In any other circumstance, it would be weird, but at the same time, she knew that Samuel's brother started the whole thing as a marketing strategy. Granted, that strategy was partially responsible for the fact that Leah was dating Samuel again, but it was still somewhat ridiculous.

All the same, Liv laughed. "He does. My cousin won't admit, but she hates it."

"Hates the name? Hates..."

"The way it was managed, initially," Liv replied, knowing that he'd get it. "It created crowds that he wasn't able to handle."

"I see," he replied, and she could see the gears running through his head. "Yeah. Something like that in the circumstances he was most likely appearing in would probably be a crowd control hazard without some kind of protection. And now?"

"Now she just hates it because she thinks it belittles him." Which if nothing else was the best way of describing Leah and Samuel's relationship. But that was for later, not now.

Now? Now was the time for her to bask in the sun of Artur's smile and the way it made her feel. Hand in hand, sharing a bit of herself, and maybe, building something with a foundation for a shoulder to cry on.

The man was an enigma wrapped in a riddle, and if she took the time to think about it, Livvy had no idea whether she or her heart were going to survive him.

THE NEXT MORNING, Artur received a text.

Meet us at the JHPA headquarters.

The GPS said he was heading to an office building in Briarwood, in a new development area that Artur had sneaking suspicions he'd recognize the second he pulled in. There were cars in the parking lot, but he didn't take the second to look at them, though he did head upstairs to the building.

It was a short elevator ride as he ran through the items he expected to discuss with Asher, knowing there were a bunch of them. JHPA participation, some local mentorship events. And probably Liv, considering Asher was dating her cousin.

One of them.

The elevator doors opened, only to reveal Liv standing there, just by the elevator. Gorgeous. He wanted to thread his fingers through her hair. He settled for a smile.

"You ready?" Liv asked as he walked into the antechamber just outside the elevator.

He shrugged. "For most things," he replied. "Not sure what this is going to be." Which was true, considering he had a feeling who was going to show up for the second half.

She laughed. That laugh was going to be the death of him.

"Let's do this," she said as she opened the door to the offices.

"You guys ready?" said a familiar voice. Well. Not that familiar.

Artur had seen Ash Mendel during his playing days, and had been out of the country when Ash retired. But the touch of gray in the man's hair and the slight softening of the shoulders were the only real changes he could spot.

"Nice to see you," he said.

"Nice to see you too, Artur. Liv?"

"Hey, Ash," Liv said with a grin. "Shall we sit down?"

They headed across the office to a conference room, and Ash took out a bunch of papers and passed them over.

He skimmed the agenda, and the background information on the local mentorship program.

"This is for part two," Asher said as Artur looked up. "My co-founder will show up for the second part and this agenda."

Artur smiled; based on the tight format of the agenda and the bits of information it had, he had a strong suspicion who the co-founder was.

And most likely, he was a mutual friend.

"First part," Asher continued. "I see you've got some kind of schedule settled?"

"We have a preliminary, two of them actually, that we're looking at." Liv in full mayor mode replied before passing the pages they'd prepared after meeting with Sarah to Ash.

"And I see a few places the JHPA can play along," Ash replied, still clearly focusing on the papers. "The winter sports expo if the high school goes through with it, and some of the players can work with the youth group."

But he could see the sparks flying in Liv's eyes, the words on their way out.

"What about the blessings?" Liv asked. "I mean maybe some of the players can come and light candles with the town some of the nights?"

Artur watched the dynamic between them, prepping to step in before Asher nodded. "I like this idea. A lot. I think, depending on schedules, it's important to have some of the players on site, celebrating the holiday even as this is an event co-sponsored by the Empires."

Which was a cue if he'd ever seen one, but at the same time he was going to show his support for an idea and person he agreed with, cue or no cue. "I can see what I can do on that end," he said. "A gentle push about diversity and holidays and the meaning behind what this is."

"Good," Asher said. Was there relief in his voice? "Thank you. I appreciate it."

"Not a problem," he said. "Anything else you want to

cover before…"

There was a squeak of a door hinge, and then footsteps.

Very familiar footsteps.

"Ash, Mayor…poker this week?"

He laughed, and if he'd seen people stunned before, he couldn't be even more surprised at the expressions on both Liv and Asher's faces.

"I think I might be able to," Artur managed, knowing the completely indirect invitation was, in fact, for him. "But not sure."

Jacob nodded, looked at him; he'd known Jacob long enough to realize that this was an inspection. An 'are you okay, is there something I can see that's wrong?' But a moment later, he smiled. "Good. Glad you're settling back in."

"I know…" Liv managed, trying to figure out what was going on.

"Excuse me," Jacob interrupted, putting his hand out to Liv, clearly having decided to take control of the situation instead of letting small bits of information trickle out. "Jacob Horowitz-Margareten. New part-time Briarwood resident, boss of the best project manager ever and partner on the local mentorship program."

"Nice to officially meet you," she said, taking his hand.

He let the hand go before sitting down and looking up at Asher. "So what are we looking at here?"

Asher passed Jacob the event schedule. "I like this," he

said. "What were you thinking of; a pre-party of some sort? Fundraiser while everybody is paying attention to the joy of Hanukkah?"

"That sounds good," Asher said.

"It's a way to involve the community more," Liv said. "I'm in favor of it."

"Maybe using the model of the dreidl project, and with a few local artisans designing and auctioning off dreidls?" Jacob added. "Proceeds going to whoever we want?"

"Artisans? We don't have that kind of time," Liv said. "Designing dreidls could be time-consuming."

Artur shook his head. "Your cousin's boyfriend the sofer and his group of friends might be convinced to put their Pictionary pencils down."

Liv snorted; thankfully she wasn't the only one. "You're right. And if we spin this as an event for the community, for the mentorship program, centered around local product Samuel Levine and his hand-picked creatives, it might be something."

"As long as you don't mention the fact that Isaac is responsible for the famous Hollowville Menorah," Jacob said.

Now it was his turn to snicker. "Yep."

"And that's the event done. We can schedule either before or after the Multi Day Event Cycle or installation, or whatever you're calling it, starts. Keep me posted on who says yes and who says no. Now the small party." Jacob turned to Liv. "You're going to come and talk to the mentees before this big event?"

Liv nodded. "That's the plan." And then she turned to Artur. "Do you want to come with?"

Artur nodded. "Sounds like a good idea."

"Good answer."

Of course it was. Because he couldn't think of anything else. "Let me know the day you're going, and I'll go with you."

"Good," Jacob said. "Asher, we have business. Artur, I'll text you poker details. Mayor, it was a pleasure."

And as quickly as they came in, they headed out. Artur knew there were going to be questions, and all he had to do was prepare to answer them.

LIV LEFT THE office having gone through the most fascinating, and strange, meeting of her life. "I don't know if that was a good thing or a bad one," she said as she headed into the street.

Artur didn't seem very perturbed by anything, whether it was his job or demeanor. Knowing him at this point, it could possibly mean both.

"I think it was productive," Artur replied. "We got support from the JHPA, which is important, and the mentorship program has that event, which I'm thinking is the kickoff event for the..." he paused, and she watched his hands move, elegant fingers grabbing words out of the air "…whatever you're calling this."

"And you got dragged into two events that you neither knew were coming nor planned?"

He laughed, as if her insinuation was that predictable. "One I expected and of course I'm going to the mentorship program. And the other? The poker? If it comes to fruition, it's just…" he paused again, and she wondered what he was going to say "…Jacob's version of claiming me in front of Asher, and supporting you in the process."

"And he's…Judith's boss," Liv managed, "which is…wow."

Artur's eyes were twinkling now. "Man's a hurricane if you're not prepared."

Liv wasn't, but she wasn't going to tell him that. "Is there anybody he doesn't like?"

Artur gestured toward a tiny noodle shop in the shopping center with the building, and Liv nodded. "He and Isaac don't get along. But Isaac is a singular personality who doesn't like people, and he and Jacob have stepped on each other's toes."

Isaac…one of Samuel's artist friends? Yep. Had to be. And also the guy who built that gorgeous metal menorah in Hollowville, at least that's what she could remember. But all she could think about, aside from the udon she was about to order, was the tangled web of connections that she and Artur shared.

And Saturday.

Already there were dynamics that she needed to watch, toes she couldn't step on. "So, what am I walking into on Saturday?"

Having ordered their udon, they moved into a private booth, sitting across from each other. Artur grabbed the chopsticks and separated the pieces of wood, "There's going to be a good group of people, a lot of them close friends."

Now she raised an eyebrow. "Of each other? Of you? Do I need a map? Should I bring reinforcements?"

He dropped the chopsticks immediately, his hands up, palms out, as if he was suddenly the conversation traffic cop. "It's not going to be that kind of thing, I mean where you need reinforcements," he clarified. "You can bring people, but I promise, the will be no pressure, personal or professional."

She nodded. Okay. This felt better. But still, what was this event really supposed to be? "So, this isn't pressure for me, or isn't supposed to be. What is this for you? A family reunion?

He laughed, picking up the chopsticks again as the teapot arrived. Hot tea got poured into the tiny cups that sat next to them.

"I'm friendly with old-fashioned nudniks, or busybodies," he replied as the steam rose from their cups. "My friends don't want to judge you; they just want to *see* you. See what you're like…and what you're like with me."

Rather, she thought, as she put her hands around the cup, seeking the warmth it provided, what she *saw* in him. Okay. That made sense.

"So, who are these people? I mean…don't need names, social security numbers and all of that jazz…"

Artur snorted and put his own hands around his cup. "What classified information do you need, Mayor?"

Liv laughed. God she adored bantering with this guy. "Maybe their professional states?"

He didn't answer immediately, but he nodded "Okay, sure. Is there any particular reason for this briefing?"

What was her reasoning? Why was she asking him these questions? Aside from wanting to know more about him and his friends, but that couldn't be the only information she wanted.

And then it hit her. "I'm trying to figure out who I can bring with me."

He raised an eyebrow. "It's a debate?"

She nodded. "Different people would have different advantages."

"Makes sense," he said. "You wouldn't bring someone that you didn't think could fit in."

"Or couldn't enjoy themselves."

"Right. Well," he continued. "At this party there will be: the host of the party—the guy who created the barbecue menu for Levitan's, and his wife who is a Meal Network host—*Batya's Journeys* I think the show is."

"I think we may have gone to the same school for a very, very brief period of time," Liv managed. "I was little and she was older, but they talk about her in the alumni magazine."

"It's possible," Artur replied. "You went to Schecter?"

Liv nodded. "For a number of years. My sister and I. Anyway, so?"

"Right. So next is the hurricane you just met, and his equally formidable wife—a museum curator. Then there's the Hanukkah consultant and her husband Isaac."

"The Isaac that Jacob doesn't like?"

"That would be the one," he said with a grin. "Then you have our friend the attorney and her girlfriend possibly of the moment, possibly more. And then my buddy Leo and his wife, who is friendly with a bunch of people in Briarwood."

She nodded. There was an interesting group of people coming to this event, and she wondered what was going on. "Based on what you told me," she began over slurps of her noodles, "my thought is that if I bring either of my cousins, they will be either pulled into a work thing or intimidated and not enjoy themselves."

"Aaah. Okay. So then what or who's your plan?"

"My sister," she replied as he signed a credit card receipt she didn't realize he'd gotten.

"It's fine," he said quickly. "If you're concerned, it's a business expense."

Whether he actually meant he considered their outing a business expense or whether he was just saying that, who knew. But either way. "Thank you."

He nodded after he passed the plastic tray over to the waiter, taking a break to slurp his own noodles. "Tell me about your sister."

"Her name's Naomi, and she's younger than I am."

"What does she do?"

"She's an event planner, mostly weddings but some other parties, corporate or otherwise. Anyway, she's uninvolved with politics and sports, but she likes events and likes being around people."

"Well," he said. "Looking forward to meeting her."

"Whether you'll say that after the event remains to be seen." She said as they dove in to lunch before finishing and heading out of the restaurant. "See you on Saturday?"

"See you on Saturday."

And their goodbyes were done, leaving her free to wave and head back to her office, to the work she had waiting that had nothing to do with him or with Hanukkah.

Chapter Seventeen

ARTUR PUT DOWN the last case of wine within his vicinity, having stacked wine, soda, beer, chips and who knew what else. He'd been lifting boxes and bags all afternoon.

Thankfully, he wasn't the only one; Abe had enlisted the entire quiz show group to help, after all. Leo was doing something in the back, Sapna was organizing the drinks behind the bar, and Claire and her girlfriend were on snack duty. Batya was helping Abe with prep, of course.

It had been a nice afternoon; Liv had been right about how this group of friends didn't really need a reunion considering how deeply everybody was in each other's pockets. And Claire's new girlfriend was nice.

Except Artur couldn't help but stare at any timepiece that came into his line of sight. A watch, an electronic assistant; anything. This impatience was doing him absolutely zero good. And between bringing boxes and bags from the landing spot to her girlfriend behind the snack table, Claire had been staring at him for the last ten minutes. Undertones of 'are you okay' were extremely clear in her eyes.

He was fooling nobody.

Which meant he needed to get to the one person who could talk him off the ledge and prevent him from going splat before Liv got there.

He headed toward the porch where Claire was standing with her girlfriend.

"You okay?" Claire asked as he approached the pair, clearly visibly relieved that she had finally asked the question she wanted to.

He nodded, yanked back to reality. "Need a break from this, so I'm going to try and relieve Batya for a while." At least that least that was what he intended.

Claire nodded, grinning, "Abe definitely needs something," she said.

And he could believe it; Batya had been on a tear since breakfast; there was something about hosting a gathering that threw her a little off her game.

Abe just fell into his element, but to Batya, there was a difference between making barbecue and hosting people.

"And what about me?"

Claire snorted. "You look like if you see another case of wine, you'll create a typhoon of it all over everybody."

Which wasn't exactly the problem he had, but the problem he'd admit to at the moment. "You know me all too well," he told his friend. "Happy lifting."

"So how will I know who will be here to help me move this?"

He laughed. "Either I'll be back or Batya will."

Which is when he waved and headed inside in search of his friend. Of course, if he wasn't sure where Abe was, he could always follow the smell.

Barbecue meant Abe's sauce, which was as familiar as the back of his own hand. He even made it once, under pressure at the prelude to the latke fry-off when he'd been Abe's sous chef.

Now, the smoker was going and it was beautiful, filling the air with hickory joy. The smoke twined with the smells of the sauce in a beautiful hazy cloud that meandered through the open windows, and he followed it into the house and toward the kitchen.

Sauce and hickory haze marked the stage in Abe's barbecue prep where the barbecue master needed babysitting as much as the food did, a tradition as old as their adulthood. And, more specifically, the reason why they were all here, in the house he'd spent so much of his childhood in.

Abe had lived here as a kid and bought the place from his father about eight years before. His best friend had sold his Manhattan apartment when his desire to work on his barbecue was greater than his desire to live in a space as big as his thumb.

In a manner of speaking.

Lucky for his best friend, his father had been ready to sell. Artur wondered what would have happened if his parents had been ready to sell their house when Abe was ready to buy; only three years after Abe's father was.

But that was a question meant for different times, considering he didn't think he'd be able to stay in Abe's guest room if Abe lived in that house. Lucky for him, that hadn't been the case.

"Artur," Batya said as he entered the kitchen. "How goes it?"

She looked harried, slightly uncomfortable at this point. Hot despite the temperature as if she'd been dragging various objects across the house.

Did the vacuum she used for half of her cleaning spree gain weight, muscle or both? Was the house full of that much surface dust and grime?

But she'd actually asked him about his mental state, not his opinion of hers. "It goes," he finally said. "I feel like I'm going to see dancing wine cases in my nightmares."

Batya smirked. "As long as you don't cut them down, they won't multiply. Did I not teach you anything?"

Movie references. She was answering him in movie references which meant she needed an extra pick-me-up. "I didn't feed them after midnight," he replied with a shrug, playing along, "or wet them, so they're fine."

Abe's singular laugh could be heard anywhere, and it was nice to hear it now. "Too many references," his best friend said, making his presence known as he stood in front of the stove. "Both of them wonderful. Except what's going on?"

Batya looked at him, and miracle of miracles she knew

him well enough to see the cracks and dents in the armor. Both her husband's and his. Without asking. "You want to take over?"

He raised an eyebrow. "Are you still cleaning or am I in the babysitting phase?"

"If I see another bottle of cleaning solution," Batya said, "I will lose my ever-loving mind faster than someone could snap their fingers and say some random Aramaic phrase."

He laughed. Abe, thankfully, did as well. "Got it," Artur said.

"Hey," Abe said with a laugh. "Don't I get a vote?"

Batya raised an eyebrow, and she turned toward her husband. Their relationship was something he adored and felt ridiculously lucky to be able to be close to as it developed.

"He's been on front-end lifting for a while," Batya said, turning toward Abe. "You want I should give him a break?"

The look that passed between them was hard fought and wonderful. Beautiful, even. He was proud of it.

Not that he'd been directly responsible, like he was for the very first campaign he'd done all those years earlier.

But this. This was two people who couldn't figure themselves out for way too long. He'd just given them a tiny bit of guidance a few years before, and now he watched them with a sense of almost...paternal?...pride, as they grew and bloomed together.

"What's that look?" Abe said.

"What look?" Artur replied, knowing that if he actually

admitted how he felt about their relationship, neither of them would know what to say.

"Isn't the normal response to say something weird, like get a room?"

"Have I ever been normal?" Artur asked, knowing the response as well as he knew his friend.

"Nope. And that's why we adore you and that weird smile on your face." Batya grinned, pointing at her husband with a thumb. "So why is it you want to go back here with him, exactly?"

"Because," Abe said, scrutiny in his eyes as clear as the smirk Artur had worn. "If I had to guess, my best friend just happens to be removing himself from a situation where aside from lifting and sorting boxes, he'd been staring at the driveway and driving himself crazy as he looks for a particular guest to arrive."

"Too many rabbits staring at watches for my taste," he confirmed with a smile.

"As long as there aren't any pumpkins riding horses you're fine," Batya said.

"That's North Hollowville, and I'm unconcerned," Artur replied, wrapping himself in the banter. "If we have a ghostly writer asking how a pumpkin looks in the dark, then we have a problem."

Abe shook his head. "You are hopeless."

"You know you love us," Batya replied, grinning.

This was perfect. Except for the…thing he saw out of the

corner of his eye. It took up a bit of the corner of the back-yard, on the opposite side of the smoker.

What was it?

A hut. A hut with lights and vegetables on the roof.

But why?

The harvest holiday of Sukkot had passed, as had the cel-ebration his friends had where they erected the sukkah, the hut in question, before he'd started working in Briarwood.

"Speaking of hopeless," he said, pointing at the glass doors and their view of the sukkah. "Why is your sukkah still up?"

Batya grinned. "We can leave the sukkah up till Thanks-giving," she sang, echoing a popular parody song. "This is our house; being Jewish is cool."

"Please tell me it's not staying up till November," Abe said. Of course.

"Hey," Batya said with a grin. "People leave Christmas lights up till January. We can leave a sukkah up till Novem-ber."

"But Christmas lights don't involve produce," Abe said, echoing what Artur knew to be a long-standing argument.

Batya raised an eyebrow and Artur stepped away from the conversation. "And you think the plastic lifelike items in the sukkah are more perishable than lights?"

Abe turned away from the smoker briefly, allowing Artur to see his eyes. They were bright and twinkly and excited. "Fine," he said with a laugh. "It's our, our, our,

our…custom."

Apparently this was just another act, which Artur appreciated.

"This," Batya said with a laugh of her own, "is why I love him. And why I'm leaving because it's very clear you need to consult him."

"Thanks, B," he replied. "Very much appreciate it."

And she left the room, leaving him and Abe alone.

AT FIVE P.M., Liv stretched, and put down the book she'd been reading about the history of the county legislature, knowing Naomi would arrive shortly.

She headed toward the front window of her town house, and lo and behold, Naomi was at her door.

Looking gorgeous.

Not that she usually paid much attention to what she wore beyond the need to look presentable at all times. But her sister always looked more than presentable; she had an effortless sense of style that sometimes, Liv wished she had.

"So, what is this again? Where are we going?"

Naomi also tended to get right to the point, and Liv sighed. "My bad decision."

It was as if they were taking the sighing baton back and forth between each other. "But," her sister said, "if someone asks me, and I have a feeling they might, I need to know what you're calling this. Beyond your bad decision."

Words, concepts; she had them and they needed to be used. "A barbecue pop-up by the guy who set up the barbecue menu at Levitan's," Liv replied with as straight a face as she could, given the circumstances.

Naomi nodded. Then paused, an imaginary lightning bolt of discovery or remembrance flashing over her head.

Which made Liv nervous.

"Wait," Naomi said. "This is what you were talking to me about at Shabbat dinner last week, right?"

Life had been so wild that she'd managed to forget she'd confided in her sister in the first place.

That made the whole explanation and eggshells awkward as hell. And yet all the same, Liv nodded. "Yes," she said. "I took your advice and…"

"Which meant I agreed to come to the event I strongly suggested you come to. Even better. So yes. You've made a good choice, two of them."

"What choices?"

"Agreeing to go, and then inviting me."

In the silence, Liv knew something was wrong. Naomi had gotten too quiet for her own safety if not taste. "Yes?" Liv said. "Because I know you have something on your mind, and you desperately want to say it."

"You know this is just dinner, and you're going, right? What do you intend to play this off as?"

This was how she had to explain herself and the situation

without disclosing the extent to which she'd already fallen for this guy.

"What swayed me," she replied, pulling words together that hopefully made some degree of sense, "is that Artur wanted to reinforce new connections that I've been making through him that might be helpful."

There. As professional as she could make it sound, as unemotional and impersonal as it could be.

Naomi raised an eyebrow.

It was a tell of her sister's; she'd said something Naomi didn't believe. "And does he know you're thinking of this as a networking event? Not just for this event, but for events in the future. That he's introducing you to contacts, not friends? In his hometown?"

It turned out the thing Naomi didn't believe was all of it. Which meant Liv needed another way of explanation, courtesy of the man himself. "He knows I might," she said. "He actually suggested something like it, in the event I was nervous about seeming unprofessional or untoward."

"Untoward is out of one of Melanie Gould's books...or Penina Alton Schraders," Naomi replied, rattling off authors she'd recently started reading. "And it would sound worse, except it does in fact sound like it was tailor-made by this guy because he knows you enough."

Which was a compliment wrapped in an insult and par for the course for her sister. "That sounds worse than it actually is."

"It's an out," Naomi replied. "An excuse, which you're grabbing onto as tightly as you can so that you don't have to admit to having feelings of any sort. Which is fine."

"It is?" Liv managed, surprised at her sister's easy acceptance of the statement. "Why?"

"Don't look a gift horse in the mouth," Naomi replied, running a hand through her long dark hair. "But what I will say, is that in this case, actions speak more than one thousand words. This picture is going to be fascinating."

She smiled, but then the phrasing brought her to her earlier dilemma. Jeans, a sweater, nice earrings. Perfect for fall. And yet.

She needed an expert opinion, and Naomi would be the ideal person to deliver it. "Speaking of pictures, I have a question for you."

Naomi raised an eyebrow. "Okay?"

This was it. Here she went, not off the deep end but ready to go. "How do I look?"

"What do you mean how do you look? You look fine—comfortable and ready to go to a barbecue."

Naomi was so nonchalant, and Liv envied that. Not always, but now, right here at this one. Because going to this really meant something. She could tell. "But…"

Naomi shook her head, and Liv knew she was in trouble. "You're playing this straight down the middle," her sister said. "You're casual but you have a full face of makeup on. So I'm not quite sure what you're trying to do?"

Liv sighed. How could she explain herself to her sister? How could she express exactly how she felt without telling her.

But her sister knew her well enough to stand in front of her, looking earnest, like she genuinely wanted to hear what Liv had to say. "I want to look…nice but professional, but not too professional."

Which was enough for Naomi to translate. "Right. Fifty date, fifty professional. Okay." At which point Naomi grabbed her hand and dragged her into the bathroom and turned on the light.

"Just a little to zhuzh you up a bit."

Liv nodded, because she knew better.

This was, of course, part of Naomi's job. Translating clients' beauty standards and random inquiries into event-ready looks. And she put herself into her sister's hands, opening and closing her eyes, turning her head, bending down and then lifting up. Liv felt like she was in a workout video.

But this was different.

After what felt like ten minutes or ten hours, Liv wasn't touched and hadn't moved, which meant Naomi must have been looking critically or something to that effect.

"Okay," Naomi finally said. "Look."

And look she did, in the horrible mirror in the bathroom she had refused to change over the period she'd lived in the town house. But it served its purpose, at least this time highlighting the work her sister had done.

Even she could see it.

The changes were subtle but made all the difference: the subtle additions to the hair and the makeup Naomi had made helped her achieve the look she wanted.

Someone going on what felt like a professional date that wasn't as professional as she was trying to make herself believe. "This is wonderful," she managed.

"Thank you, ma'am," her sister quipped. "You look gorgeous."

She wouldn't go that far, but nice was enough, and for that moment, she felt just right. She definitely owed her sister.

"Thank you," she managed.

Naomi nodded, pride in her expression. "You're welcome." And then she paused, and Liv met her sister's eyes.

"What?" she asked.

"Are you ready?"

Liv looked at her watch and nodded. "Yeah. Ready as I'll ever be."

Naomi followed Liv into the cold winter night, their destination Liv's car and the pop-up in Rivertown. Liv was about to unlock the car when Naomi's phone buzzed.

Her sister looked down before looking up, an indecipherable expression on her face. "Hold on," she said.

Liv nodded, hoping desperately that this wasn't one of Naomi's work emergencies; the work of a party planner was never done. But the phone call was quick, and when Naomi ended the call, something like a sigh emerged from her sister's mouth.

"What's up?" Liv asked. "Nothing too serious I hope?"

"Not really," Naomi replied. "We just need to wait a little bit."

Liv raised an eyebrow. "Why?"

At which point, whether in answer to her question or not, a horn honked. Liv looked up only to see a gray SUV pulling into the complex. "Huh?"

"I couldn't stop him," Naomi said.

Was that fear? Nerves…what?

"Who?" Liv asked.

"It's fine," Naomi answered, sounding ridiculously frazzled all of a sudden. "He's my guest?"

Liv had no idea what was happening and had less when the car pulled up to where they stood, and the window rolled down, revealing Jason, the closest thing that Asher had to a little brother. And one of the owners of Greenblatt's Knish Shop.

What? Was he spying on behalf of the chamber of commerce? Of Asher? Or…

But instead of acting like this was out of the ordinary, Naomi grinned in his direction.

"We ready?" he asked as he rolled down the window. "And this is a protection mission," he continued. "We don't truck with certain members of the chamber. I've got too many contacts to deal with that. So. You're safe."

Naomi blinked and shook her head, as if none of what Jason said had made sense. But more importantly, Liv did understand.

"I guess we are," Liv said.

Liv got into the back seat of the car behind Naomi, who was in the front seat babbling at Jason in an extremely familiar manner that was puzzling in a way Liv couldn't not notice; she was aware that something interesting was going on between the two of them.

At some point, she'd ask Judith if she'd seen any of this...growing relationship between Jason and Naomi, but if she had to guess, the person who would know would be Leah.

Leah, who Naomi actually confided in.

But for now, the order of the day was pondering how this whole party was going to go. Meeting Artur's friends, navigating complicated webs of people. As they pulled her and Artur together, it worried her that they pulled them apart.

Chapter Eighteen

AFTER A GOOD conversation with Abe, at about six thirty, it was determined that the time had arrived for the show to begin. All of the setup crew from the quiz bowl team had arrived, including Sapna who'd dropped off her and Leo's daughter at a friend's house for the night.

Now, the stage was set.

Sapna was pouring drinks to keep herself from the snack table that Batya was manning, Claire was preparing the dessert table, with her girlfriend Natalie in tow. Which meant he and Leo were sent to the front. Their job was to direct the arriving cars toward good spots. They wore safety vests with fluorescent strips and carried flashlights.

So far, it had gone well—there were open parking spaces along the street and the neighbors had been notified; some of them had offered either driveway space or space in front of their houses in exchange for some food.

Which was a price that Abe had been very willing to pay.

By 7 p.m., the first bunch of guests had arrived; Sarah and Isaac as well as Jacob and Anna went to the back, trying to help in some way. Tony Liu, an attorney who worked with Jacob and his wife Charlotte, a chef, restaurateur and baker who got to know Batya and Abe through the Latke Fry-off, were also there. If he had to guess, Charlotte was probably trying to help with, if not take over, the dessert table.

"It's not work," Charlotte had said as she carried the cake she'd been asked for.

But in the back of his mind, Artur inventoried cars and guests; a partner from Abe's old accounting firm even showed up.

And yet Liv still wasn't there.

Until, that was, an unfamiliar gray SUV arrived, the driver following Leo's flashlight toward a space down the street.

"Must be her," he thought to himself.

"Did you not complain about house duty because you were waiting for someone to show up?" Leo, who had returned to their post after directing the car, decided to respond to something Artur hadn't actually said out loud.

But with his luck he'd actually managed to say it out loud, which meant he had to own it. "What if it was?"

Leo shook his head. "You ridiculous buffoon," he said, an inch away of rubbing his head. "And you know that *if* I don't say it, someone else will."

"Yes," Artur replied. "I'm well aware that you're not the only person willing to discuss my frailties and foibles."

"Good." Leo clapped his shoulder, punctuating the

statement. "You deserve to be discussed and analyzed in all ways and forms. Because it's important for your existence and morality."

Artur shook his head. "Of course it is." Because that was the sort of interrogation that came with friends who mattered. Who cared about him, and who he cared about in return. He'd kept them both in line over the years; he knew they'd do the same and didn't expect any less.

And when Liv walked up the driveway behind a couple, he found himself shoving his hands in his pockets, not from the cold, but from the want of something to do with his fingers.

"Go get the girl you've been waiting for," Leo said, jabbing him in the back like they were in fifth grade, trying to do something ridiculous.

The other part of having friends like Leo was they understood your language—spoken and unspoken, which is why he didn't smack him like they were ten when Leo said to go find…her.

Of course, that was the moment where she stood in front of him, gorgeous under the lights in a way that took his breath away. "Hi," he managed when he could pull himself together.

"Hi," she said.

She was someone who usually had a bunch of words to use in most situations, but here, standing in front of him, he could see she didn't.

Which meant he had to jump into the conversation and make something clear before she headed into the backyard. "I'm apologizing in advance for this."

She raised an eyebrow, and he hoped she wasn't going to jump into whatever car she came in and leave before she entered the party for real. But now it was his time to watch her pull herself together, to reel in her emotions and put them away where they belonged.

"For what?" she asked.

"For my friend's immature behavior caused by the inability to not introduce you."

The noise he'd heard from her was a strange one; he'd guess it was a combination of a laugh and a snort. Or something. "Well," she said, clearly taking the reins of the situation. "Olivia Nachman. Mayor of Briarwood, invited guest. You can call me Liv."

"Leo Fratelli," Leo interjected, taking the offered hand like the gentleman he was capable of being. "Friend of this dude, and friend of the dude whose house this is."

There was silence, and the Look on Liv's face was…

He had to do something.

Quickly.

But his friend was smart; they'd known each other forever.

"No matter what other capacity you may know me in," Leo said with a smile, "this friendship with this guy, is the most important one."

"I've known this guy since we were in fifth grade," Artur interjected, somehow mirroring the words Leo had yelled back in front of the Pasta Station. "He didn't participate in the latke fry-off."

"But I did introduce the final challenge," Leo interjected.

"Don't mention that challenge," Artur said before turning to Liv. "That was the one Abe lost on. He had to be brought back by the people's…"

"Ricotta latke," Leo said with a large grin on his face. "I own Fratelli's restaurant in Rivertown and we do a Hanukkah menu every year in conjunction with the Hollowville Festival and Rivertown's events."

"And yes," Artur said, adding the thing he'd asked Leo randomly a few weeks before, "he's willing to extend the discount to those who enter with a Briarwood stamp. Or a receipt or a ticket from some event that you and he can figure out later."

She blinked, surprised but the smile on her face was welcome. And a relief. "Thank you," she said.

"You're welcome. I'm a good guy," Leo said. "Better than he thinks I am."

Which made Artur snort.

"You guys are so close," Liv said, clearly falling back into the situation, as if Leo had managed to successfully diffuse the tension mentions of Briarwood had created. "And it's nice to meet you."

Which was when the couple who'd been behind them

joined them. "So, Liv," interjected another voice, "should you introduce us?"

"Yes," Liv said, smiling. "This is my sister Naomi and…"

"Jason," the guy interjected, giving Leo a look. "Jason Greenblatt of the Michigan Greenblatts. And of Manhattan and Briarwood." He grinned. "I don't truck with the chamber either. Too many ears here watching out for—" he pointed a backward thumb at Liv "—her."

"My best friend since fifth grade," Leo said. "Nothing is more important."

And just like that, as a peace and a boundary was established, conversations about the chamber of commerce and who deserved that information forgotten in favor of the joy of knishes, Artur found himself relieved.

And nervous, knowing the rest of the night still lay ahead.

LIV WASN'T SURE what to make of the night; it was fun for sure. The food was amazing, and the people were lovely. Batya had in fact been an older student at Schechter when she was there.

"You were in Mrs. Kuflik's class when you were there, right?"

She nodded. "I was," she said. In first grade, of course.

Where they had the bridge ceremony between the first

graders and the eighth graders.

And that's why Batya looked familiar; she'd been the eighth grader who had spent time with her when she was in first grade. It was fun to catch up with her. "Keep me posted," Batya said. "I want to know everything."

"Once life slows down for both of us we need to grab coffee."

"I'd like that," Batya had said.

Her husband was also lovely; Liv could see the friend that had saved Artur as a fifth grader; the guy was all heart.

"Just be careful," Abe had said. "There's a very, very huge heart behind the hall-of-mirrors exterior."

She nodded. "I will," she said, taking the warning for what it was. "You don't have to spend much time to see it."

Sarah, the Hanukkah consultant, was excited to see her again. "You know what'll be great?" she said as Jason came back to either spy on them or add to the conversation.

"What?"

Sarah turned to Jason and grinned widely in his direction. "Knishes in the food area during the event cycle. Maybe a knish-making demonstration…"

He looked between them, blinking as if he hadn't expected the conversation to make that kind of turn. "What do you mean, I…"

"Oh, come on," Sarah said. "You're coming over here for a reason and I just wanted to make you part of the conversation."

"So, you're asking me about Briarwood Hanukkah business now?"

Sarah nodded, and Liv grinned. "I always want to talk Hanukkah business, especially when I have a willing listener, and a participant who hasn't made himself available."

Whether Liv was actually willing or whether she was just enjoying the conversation on a late October night, she wasn't sure. But she was there, and it was obvious Jason had been thwarted by Sarah and her plans. "Very," she said.

"So, you want a collab with the restaurants or do you want a special Hanukkah item in the vendor...whatever you're doing in the center of Briarwood?"

Liv thought for a second and grinned. "Both," she said, enjoying Jason's discomfort as the payment he got for spying. "That would work perfectly; something both inside and outside of Briarwood, to tie the town and the celebration to the heritage of both the town and the holiday."

Jason nodded. "When your plans are a bit more concrete, let me know," he said, pointing to Artur where he stood in the distance. "But I'll consult with my brother who's deeper into the restaurant than I am. I have a Hanukkah party to cater, one which is going to have a few dreidls."

So, Jason was going to cater the Hanukkah party Jacob Horowitz-Margareten was throwing for the benefit of the mentorship program. "Got it."

"Yes. You'll be there?"

She nodded. "Looking forward to it."

And suddenly yet another string fell into place between her and Artur, a connection that felt good, she decided as she headed toward the drinks table.

Which was when she was stopped by a rather tall gentleman. "Hello?"

"Hi," he said, grinning. "Isaac Lieberman. You met my wife."

And this was the Isaac Jacob didn't like. "Nice to meet you, too. I'm Liv. Liv Nachman."

"Nachman...sounds familiar. Are you related to..."

There was an extended pause and Liv couldn't figure out who or what he was going to ask her about.

"Leah." He paused again, looking at her with the expression of someone who is convinced they may have either made the wrong choice or asked someone the wrong question. "I know it's a common name...but..."

"It's fine," Liv said. "She's my cousin."

"Oh good." Isaac shook his head. "Sometimes I can be counted upon to say the worst things and because it took you so long to reply, I thought I did this time, but I'm glad to know I didn't. Anyway, have you met her boyfriend?"

Again, she nodded. "Samuel is lovely," she said.

And then a lightning bolt went off in her head.

Her husband's part of the Brooklyn art crew that includes a sofer...

"Tell him I said hello," Isaac continued, oblivious of the web of connection coming to life in her head, even more so than it had before.

"I will," she said. "Next time I see him."

"Good."

And as Isaac headed off, she found herself alone, with a drink and a snack, knowing that this was definitely a wonderful evening.

All thanks to Artur.

Who was…*somewhere.*

And Liv needed to find him.

"SHE'S LOOKING ANTSY." Abe, of course. "Looking like she's having fun, but a bit antsy."

Artur nodded. "Yeah. I just…"

"Let me get this straight," Abe said shaking his head. "You heard the advice I gave you before this started, and then decided to ignore it completely? Is that the gist of it?"

The advice he gave before…

Right. The advice Abe had given him before he'd headed out with Leo on parking duty. In front of the smoker, in front of the side dishes.

"You're going to be tempted to leave her to her own devices," Abe said. *"So she can give in to her own impulses about networking and what she thinks she's here for."*

"And that's not a good idea?"

Abe shook his head. "You've invited her here. Yes. Let her network and meet people, but don't leave her alone completely.

That's not what this is for."

"So what is it for?"

The expression on Abe's face would have, in childhood when both of them were much smaller, heralded some kind of shaking, some moment where Abe grabbed his shoulders and shook, as if the motion would somehow get the brain to where Abe thought it should be.

But now, only the expression remained, a phantom limb of childhood experiences and learned conversations.

And moments where lessons were expected.

"You don't know?" Abe asked, incredulity lacing his words like caramel on ice cream. "You need to go check on her. You need to find her."

She was doing business, finding her feet. If he stopped her too early, he'd lose her. "But…"

"No buts. She's not drowning," Abe said. "But she's not relaxed either. She seems like she's looking for something, and I'll bet it's not a thing she's looking for but a *you*."

"She's not ready… I…"

"What do you think she isn't ready for? Why do you have to wait?"

And that was the question, wasn't it? Something he had to answer honestly soon, or deal with the consequences. Because as he turned around, there she was.

"Hey, I thought I'd find you here."

And if he wasn't ready now, he never would be. "Hey," he said. "Do you want to debrief?"

She blinked. "Okay?"

"Come on," he said offering his hand. And as he took it, he went toward the one place where he thought they'd have some degree of privacy without leaving the backyard.

The sukkah.

Chapter Nineteen

L IV FOLLOWED ARTUR toward the structure, belatedly realizing that it was a sukkah.

"What's going on?" she asked.

"Wanted to talk to you away from the eyes of most people in the crowd," he said. "Eyes and ears and all."

He wanted privacy. He wanted to get her alone. But she needed to be clear. "And your words are for my ears only?"

He nodded.

"Doubt that would happen with this crowd," she said with a smile, knowing how closely his friends watched him, not to mention how Naomi was. "But it's a nice thought."

He shrugged, but he didn't seem overly concerned. "I figure if we go in here, we have an illusion that we're the only people in there, or at least unless someone reeeally wants to busybody their way into our conversation."

She nodded. That made sense no matter what he wanted to tell her.

Or not tell her, for that matter.

But the kicker was that he'd been keeping some kind of distance from her.

Why?

They hadn't said words or had the conversation they'd planned to have, so maybe he'd drawn boundaries until they said words?

But he wanted privacy. He'd asked her here, out of sight and earshot from the rest of the crowd, protected by a barrier of...a hut with an open roof, vegetables and fruit hanging within reach.

Was this...?

She didn't know.

But she'd followed him anyway.

"How are you doing?" he asked as they stepped inside the walls of the sukkah. "Is there anything you need? Anything you've been doing?"

"You want a debrief?" she asked, not being able to help the grin. "I mean this is partially a chance for me to network."

He nodded. "A businessy place to do business for a mayor from two towns over."

"Maybe. Or the new legislator for a few legislative districts over, depending on which title you want to use." She wondered if clarifying was the right move; at that point, she was on shaky ground.

Which meant things that grounded her were what she needed; not the uncertain and unfamiliar title that felt like she was reaching beyond her grasp.

But it didn't seem to faze him.

"Either way," he said. "How has it been going?"

"Good," she said, being entirely unable to keep from smiling at him. "I've met some interesting and cool people, who seem really nice and also great business contacts."

He nodded. "My intention exactly."

And then she realized something. This was his best friend's house, and he seemed, from afar at least, comfortable with everybody in a way that she wasn't used to seeing from him.

He'd pulled this together, giving her reasons she could come, and created a safe space for her to do so, riding that fine line between business and pleasure in a way she could rationalize.

With people he could trust.

"You have a very, very cool inner circle," she said. "Thank you for letting me in."

He blinked, the rest of the surprise transforming his face as it did every time she said something he didn't expect or went somewhere he didn't expect her to.

"You're welcome," he finally said, making it clear the leap of logic was welcome. "And I'm so very lucky to know them...and you."

The pause, the slight tremble in his voice.

He wasn't the only one who was nervous. She could see it now as he stood within touching distance. There was a bottle of wine and two glasses he must have snuck into the sukkah before she'd found him.

"Do you want a drink?

She shook her head. "Later," she said unable to keep the tremble out of her own voice. "We...we... I think we have to talk first."

He nodded, but that nervous energy was visible in every move he made. His hand shook slightly when he reached out. Dear God she wanted to hug him. This cool, confident man was nervous.

And she was responsible.

Liv actually thought he was going to reach for the glass, but his hand went right past it, grabbing for the display of vegetables that were on the table behind her.

What...

"Broccoli."

Now it was her turn to blink in surprise, shock.

What the heck was he doing holding the leafy green vegetable, or at least a pretty good facsimile of it? The vegetable sat in his hands, long fingers flashing greenery in her face. "What?"

"A tradition," he said. "In certain Eastern European countries, the broccoli is a symbol of love and romance."

Aaah.

"I see," she said, the amusement at his line of conversation overpowering the fear that sat in the pit of her stomach.

Not fear of him, exactly. But fear of the situation and what she might...no. Not might.

What she was going to do.

Where this was going to lead, and how powerless she was to stop it.

"So," she managed, trying to take the situation seriously. "What do you do with it? Put it under your pillow?"

"No," he said, stepping closer to her, closing the distance between them.

Yep. She was in trouble.

Deep trouble, because any resolve she'd managed to pull together was gone and showing no signs of return.

But she needed to keep an expression on her face that demonstrated she took this, and him, seriously. "Wear it under your clothing? Near certain parts of your body to inspire their function?"

This time, she could see the twitch by the corner of his mouth, as if he was holding back laughter. The first dent in his armor she'd seen all night.

"No," he said, pushing on, his voice wrapping around her, turning her insides to jelly.

She laced her fingers together and looked up. "What then?"

He pointed upwards, to a string hanging down from the roof, a duplicate of the broccoli he'd jettisoned hanging from it.

"If you kiss under it," he said, "your relationship will be as blessed as the green of the broccoli, and gets stronger at its root."

Despite everything, despite what she knew was about to

happen, she wanted to laugh. Whether it was nervous laughter or amusement at the story he was telling, she didn't know.

But deep inside, she knew that giving in to the laughter would be a horrible idea, the moment was wrapped up in too many other things she didn't want to defuse. And so, instead, she said the first words that came into her head. "You're full of pudding."

He looked so adorably puzzled, this man who made magic of language and space for her.

This enigma wrapped in a riddle.

She wouldn't hold herself responsible for what she was about to do; it was natural, necessary now that he stood in front of her in a place that felt more private than it was. But he'd opened that door, created that space.

And prepared himself for failure.

He needed her, and if she was going to be honest with herself, she needed him too.

So, she kissed him.

Which shouldn't have felt so inevitable, and yet it was. The taste of him, the way he opened up to her, the way his hands felt on her.

All of it was inevitable.

And she was doomed.

Because she didn't want to stop.

IT HAD BEEN a long time since Artur felt comfortable enough to lose himself completely in anybody or anything, and yet there he was, his entire consciousness focused on Liv. His mouth on hers, his hands on her, and his body aching, wanting to close the distance between them.

When she pulled back, he felt as if she'd taken a part of him with her. "I…"

"I liked that," she said, looking up at him. "But not just like. It felt amazing and you felt amazing and…"

"So you don't want to pretend it didn't happen?"

She shook her head. "Blaming nothing, not even the starlight. This was me…this was you…and yes."

As the words settled in his brain, the relief galloped out of him. "You're not pretending it didn't happen."

She shook her head, and the fire in her eyes reminded him of a shamash. "And you know what?"

"I don't," he said. "Tell me. I don't want to make assumptions."

"I might want to do it again," she said.

And if he was going to faint, that would be the moment.

But he didn't.

"So," she said, eyes wide and looking up at him with a mix of emotions playing across her face, drawing him in and making him want to untie the threads at the same time.

He didn't want to let go.

Unfortunately, he had to remind himself that Abe's backyard sukkah, in the middle of a party that Abe had thrown for his benefit, was NOT the place to continue exploring Liv—her mouth, or her body.

"What do you recommend we do here, Mr. Expert on…Delicate Situations?"

He shook his head, suddenly torn between his reflexive need to plan a way out that didn't harm her. And his lack of desire to leave her, because ways out and planning required distance, walls.

And he wasn't strong enough for those.

"I…don't know," he managed, his mental walls erected out of goopy modeling clay barely separated his desires for her and his need to smooth a path professionally; the way he'd done since he was twenty-one and one of his college friends had desperately needed his help.

"But what I do know," he said, grasping for clarity, "is that your sister is here and…"

"That's true," she said, moving back toward him as if he hadn't said a word. "But that isn't the delicate situation I'd like to consult you on."

"What situation would that be?" he asked, barely able to get the words out; even wrapping his mind around what was happening seemed beyond him. And the goopy clay that was starting to show holes.

"The situation where—" she put her arms around his neck "—I've decided I'm not done kissing you."

The clay fell over like melted wax, as if it had never been shaped into something akin to solid form. Words emerged out of the darkness. "Kiss me already," he said.

"Very well," she replied, her lips meeting his this time, those beautiful eyes of hers searing right through him and destroying every single wall he had ever attempted to build.

It was his turn to break the kiss. "I'm afraid that if we don't go back to the party, someone's going to send in a *search party*."

And when she nodded, she didn't pull away completely. She simply stepped away long enough to stand next to him and take his hand in hers. "Let's keep them from wasting their time," she said. "Though I don't expect them to be glad we had them call off the search."

And for the first time all night, he went into the storm of his best friends' backyard, happy, unconcerned, with a woman whom he saw something more than just a moment with.

Lucky for him, his friends were as excited about the prospect as he was. He hoped they'd leave him time to get adjusted to the situation before involving themselves further and requiring he bring her to Tuesday dinner.

Chapter Twenty

LIV HAD NEVER been around someone who fit into her life so easily. The digitization project, and time with Artur and her family filled her days after the party. It was wonderful. Until the Wednesday morning when her phone rang with an unfamiliar number.

But the number had a label: *county government*. Which meant she had to answer it. "Hello, Mayor Nachman. How can I help you?"

"Hi," said the woman on the other end. "Lacy Bryant Williams. I'm going to be your caucus leader in the County Board of Legislators, and I'm calling to welcome you to the caucus."

"Thank you," Liv said. "I'm looking forward to working with you." And she was. The caucus leader was a pretty well-known figure; she was responsible for creating proposals that initiated a bunch of changes that had happened in the county over the last few years; the cross-county train system and shuttle buses, as well as a few other important items.

"I'm looking forward to working with you as well, Mayor."

"Would you be able to attend our Hanukkah celebration here in Briarwood?"

"Hanukkah?"

Liv smiled, used to the confusion from those who lived and worked beyond the towns in the hyper local area. But she pushed forward. "Yes. In conjunction with the New York Empires the Briarwood Synagogue, and the Briarwood Temple Sisterhood. It's the first year that we're doing this, having a celebration that allows our Jewish residents to feel seen and welcomed in our community. I hope it's a tradition that the next mayoral administration continues."

"You'll have to give me more details," the caucus leader replied. "But yes. I'd love to come. Send my office the invitation and I will be there."

"Thank you," she said. "I appreciate it."

"I look forward to it," she said. "See you soon."

And as she hung up the call, Liv knew that things would be kicking into high gear. Timelines needed to be tightened; schedules needed to be fixed. She pulled out her checklist and began take notes on what needed to be done.

ARTUR BEGAN THE Wednesday morning after the party with an update call from Emily Gould-Smythe. "Good morning," Emily began. "Is everything else going well on site?"

"Actually, it is," he said, grinning. He launched into the

story of how things had progressed since the two meetings, as well as the contributions from the residents, the sisterhood, and the chamber of commerce.

Not the members of the chamber who were interested in acting as the mayor's personal watchdogs. Of course.

"That's wonderful," she said, pushing his brain and his train of thought back to the subject at hand. "I really like hearing about the way that this event has progressed since you took the reins."

"It's been great," he said, sitting back against the chair. "I think what they needed was a sympathetic ear, someone who wants to listen to them."

"You seem to know what they need, which is important."

"Speaking of interesting," he continued, not wanting to keep the conversation on him for too long. "The JHPA head is not only a local but also an Empires alum."

"Why wasn't he…?" Emily began before stopping.

He didn't know why Flaire hadn't involved him previously; he didn't want to even guess.

"You know what?" she said, probably tapping into something he'd been thinking of. "Never mind. If you don't get it; I definitely am not going to understand why he wasn't involved."

He laughed. He couldn't help himself.

"That aside," Emily continued. "I'm really looking forward to seeing how it goes on the ground."

For a second, in the guest room he'd spent a lot of his life in, he let himself dream. "I'm really excited," he managed.

"And the mayor?"

Nothing to bring himself back to earth faster than a personnel evaluation request disguised as a casual question.

But how much did he want to reveal? He clearly knew a great deal, more than he wanted to tell. So, he hedged his bets.

Professional, he reminded himself. Professional. "She's smart. Has a good head on her shoulders and a good pulse on her community. I like working with her."

"Mmmmhm."

The noise was non-committal, which was good. He didn't know what she was looking for. What kind of judgment did she want from him?

"I wondered how it would be for you, working for a woman in a position of power."

And that's what it was. Some people still had issues working for women in positions of power, to the point where they made things difficult. Emily was making sure that he wasn't one of them.

That concern was answered quite easily. "She's good at what she does," Artur replied before deciding to add a little bit. "And then she's twice as good because she's being watched by pretty much everybody nearby. As I said, she's easy to work with."

"Glad to hear that. You and I are definitely going to sit down and keep this conversation going. Think about involving female athletes in what you do for the ceremony, hm?"

Female athletes.

Interesting. As his brain started to run through the possibilities, there was a break in the silence. "Absolutely. I can talk to the JHPA head about any of the NAWHL players joining in."

"Oh," Emily said.

"What?"

"If there are any more problems that arise, with the sculpture or anything that we are responsible for providing to the Village, including the sculpture, don't tell the mayor. You presumably have a plan in place to fix any problems that may arise, so just leave her out of the loop. We've already had enough trouble with this event. We want the rest to go smoothly and want the Village residents to enjoy this and themselves without worrying about anything else."

Which was normal, usual in his line of work. NDA's between his employer and someone in the situation always could spring up to protect the employer from *something*. Usually he understood.

Except this time it left a nasty taste at the roof of his mouth that not even sour cream could clear. It found its way to his stomach, toward town hall when he'd ended the call. He and Liv had made plans to meet after the day ended, ostensibly to try out some of the special knishes Jason had persuaded his brother to make.

Instead, she wanted to try out the new ice rink. Skates were easy to find, and after they'd taken a turn, they sat on one of the benches with a bunch of knishes in hand.

But he was too distracted to really taste anything, too in his head about how to explain his life and his choices. He could feel the tips of her fingers following the space of his cheekbones through her gloves, and when he turned toward her, the expression on her face meant there was something she was about to say. "What?"

"In moments when I let myself dream," she said, "I think this may end up okay. You know?"

"What?" he asked. "What do you mean by *this*?"

"The term, the celebration, the...legacy that this event'll leave behind when I'm no longer involved in politics here in town."

And if nothing else, this was the moment when he understood, when he realized why everything was so important. The event, the cycle, whatever they were calling this, was going to be the last gift she gave to her hometown before she went off to do greater things.

"I will do my best," he said, his words a solemn vow. "No matter what it may seem like, to ensure this happens perfectly. You deserve more than this."

"I have everything I want right now," she said.

And when she kissed him, under the lights of the rink, not knowing or caring who was watching, he knew he was sunk.

He knew he was lost.

And he'd get her whatever information she needed, no matter the cost.

Chapter Twenty-One

AFTER THE PHONE call from her new caucus leader at the county legislature, things really started to kick into high gear for Liv. But at the same time, she was absolutely and fully aware that she wasn't alone. It was as if the moment under the lights at the rink had solidified...whatever was growing between her and Artur.

Instead of having a night in, Liv was supposed to meet Artur at the rather large residence that belonged to Jacob Horowitz-Margareten and his wife. It was a poker game, combined with a planning meeting for the mentorship party that would serve as a kickoff to the event cycle.

It was a good night; Judith was on her best behavior, in her perfect planner self, though there were a few looks in her direction. Samuel was in organizer mode, having taken to the dreidl auction as quickly and as easily as a duck to water. Even Jennifer Cohen was chatting along with Sarah, the Hanukkah planner, and everybody else who'd arrived.

"He's nice," Judith said with a grin before heading back to talk to her boss.

"You fit," Leah said before heading back to consult with

Asher, having let Samuel talk to the committee about the dreidls on his own.

Of course, Liv found herself flitting back and forth between conversations; planning and organizing which items would be put up for auction.

"You fit really well," said a voice she hadn't heard before.

Liv turned to meet the expression of Anna Horowitz-Margareten. "Anna Cohen," she said with a smile, holding out her hand. "I use my maiden name professionally."

Of course she did. But all the same, Liv smiled.

"I like the atmosphere you've created," Anna continued. "Both in terms of the group and in terms of the event. I will tell you that some of Artur's other friends are going to be jealous you're here tonight."

Which was not what she'd expected to hear, and so she let her surprise come through. "What?"

Anna smiled. "Your family is important to you, and I think your cousins are noticing the way you're acting."

Liv smiled back. "They are," she replied.

"But anyway," Anna continued, "with someone like Artur, who holds his cards close to the vest, his friends are family. And as you become a larger part of his life, your family and his friends will want to see more of you."

"And so they'll be asking to see me?"

"Exactly." Anna continued, "But I will say that I'm kinda glad I got you here first."

And at that point, Liv couldn't help but laugh, before

following her hostess back to the center of the party, where Artur stood waiting.

ARTUR WAS USED to switching hats and roles like a swing on a Broadway stage, but he found himself at a loss halfway through the combination meeting and poker game. Bets and antes and 'I got Bryce to make a mask and a few of the Empires are going to sign it, but also Melanie Gould is doing a dreidl and a few of her friends are going to sign it' were going to make his head explode.

Thankfully, there was a break in the action, and he headed toward a bathroom. *A bathroom.* The fact that this palatial thing was *one of* his friends' houses was still extremely overwhelming. Granted, this friend had funded the organization he'd spent the last few years working for. But still.

He saw the view of the yard space and took a breath.

"Artur," came a voice out of nowhere. It was Asher Mendel. He'd seen the man a few times during the evening, planning and organizing.

"Hey," he said. "What's up?"

"Be careful."

Immediately he was on edge; what was going on? Was it a threat? A nerve? "What?"

"My future cousin-in-law," Asher said by way of explanation.

All that did, however, was get him out of fight-or-flight mode. This was relationship- and family-related. But he was still confused. "What do you mean?"

"The family watches her like a hawk," Asher said. "Not sure how useful that'll be to you, but my fiancée told me to be careful around her mother in what I said about you."

"What you said about me?"

"Yep. My guess is that after tonight, gossip is going to fly through that family of hers—I can already see Samuel staring, and Leah making notes. Which means her family members are going to be in search of information about you, if they haven't been already. You should be prepared for invitations, and to treat things more seriously than you were going to."

That was an easy question, if Asher was asking one. Because he didn't take Liv lightly.

"She's not someone you take lightly," he replied, having pulled his words together in a way that made sense. "She's someone who has too much to lose if something goes wrong. So, you take whatever's happening with her seriously from the beginning."

"And if she's scared?"

The questions got easier and easier. "When she's ready, she'll know about my feelings and how deep they are."

Asher nodded. "Just make sure that's the only thing you're keeping from her. Trust is important to her, and there are a lot of moving parts for both of you."

Which confirmed his own suspicions after the conversation the night before and the one he'd had with his boss. He had to get some kind of plan in order to share information with her that he couldn't tell her directly.

But Asher didn't need to know that. "Thanks for the advice," he said.

"Not a problem."

And as they headed back to where everybody was gathered, thoughts ran through Artur's mind. There was a great deal that was about to happen in the next few days, and he had to make sure he was ready for all of it.

Chapter Twenty-Two

AFTER THE PLANNING meeting, Liv found herself setting into a routine with Artur. Work got done; she would call him or he would call her and they'd have lunch together. Over lunch, they'd tackle some of the problems popping up for the festival and then made time to kiss more.

When the work day was over, they'd do the things that were required of both of them; first, they'd inspect the blueprints that had been pulled together based on the suggestions given by the residents, followed by a lovely make-out session where his hands found their way under her sweater.

As construction began on some of the vendor spaces and the artists began to turn the chess tables that sat by the stage space into dreidl tables, they went to inspect the work. And then made some time for more kissing, where she discovered he was ticklish in the middle of his back.

She was enjoying every second of this.

Every hour, which meant that she was entirely not surprised when she got the phone call from her mother.

"So," her mother said, switching to video, not wasting

any time. "I've heard from Debbie."

Debbie was her aunt; Judith and Leah's mother. Debbie gave her mother gossip when she was in town.

But it wasn't a big deal.

Not at all.

"Oh really," Liv said, desperately trying to keep the tone casual. "How is she?"

"She's fine. Worried because there's been a lot of conversation in town about you being with someone."

"In town?" she asked, for clarification purposes. Because it could be her cousins or some random sisterhood informant.

"A little bit here and there," her mother replied. "Enough where it's cause for concern…in that she's worried about you."

"Okay," she said, having organized her mental ducks in the rows they required. "She's worried about what? My reputation? My life? My…"

"I don't quite care what she's worried about," her mother said. "Debbie has her own reasons, but you're my daughter. And I am worried about you."

"I don't understand," she managed, desperately trying to follow the lines of the conversation as they shifted and moved away from her.

"You keep yourself locked away because you think you need to meet some impossible standard of behavior since that awful McManus boy acted like a political campaign was the best place to air grudges he'd had since nursery school. Not to mention your father and I are aware of the double stand-ard women face, as well as the influence of the patriarchy whether it's on our own Jewish culture or on Western Christian civilization."

And there her mother went, tying the conversation to her (and her father's) field of Jewish cultural study. "Yes, Mom," she said. "My life isn't my own; I love what I'm doing, don't get me wrong, but every single thing I do matters."

"So as your mother," her mother continued, "my con-cern was the toll all of these hoops were taking on you in ways that was unhealthy. It's not right or...safe to have to do that to yourself, even though I do understand why." Her mother smiled back. "But now, now there is someone who makes you want to take chances, to be visible."

She nodded. That was true, no matter what angle it was coming from.

"Why is he different? Why are you willing to spend...quality time with him, and open your emotional boundaries? Why are you risking this?"

Why are you risking this, indeed?

Her mother's question got to the heart of her thoughts. But there was one and only one answer she could give her mother. "He gets it. He gets me."

There was a second as her mother nodded once again. "So when is he coming to Shabbas dinner?"

"I have to ask him," she said. "I don't know what his

schedule is like…"

"If he gets you," her mother said, "he'll get that this is important to both you and your family."

And when she ended the call, it was clear Liv had another call to make.

ARTUR WAS FILLED with happiness; he'd practically bounced into Abe's place on Tuesday night. Granted, Liv had been in the middle of her digitization project, so he hadn't felt so bad about leaving her behind.

But at the same time, he knew his mood was too good to last; his haze of a bubble floated too close to the sun that night, and when he'd settled into his seat, having dropped off both the wine and the dessert, Abe turned toward him.

"Nu," his best friend said. "What is this I'm hearing about you and Liv making an appearance at Jacob's for that poker night meeting I couldn't make? Especially considering I've heard neither hide nor hair of you except for breakfast and bedtime, and even that's a rare specialty."

Yep. The hazy bubble had broken, the air had been let out and it was now time to deal with the earthly consequences of his actions. He was well aware that he'd been living on gossip/inquiry-related borrowed time for weeks at this point, and he knew he was lucky. Yet at the same time, he was going to lose his mind.

Batya raised an eyebrow; she could thankfully be counted upon to defuse a situation if necessary. "It's pretty obvious what's happening, Abe," she said. "Whatever you did or put in the brisket at the party did its job."

Artur, for his part, tried not to spit out his very good, very well cooked, dinner. "Um," he managed. "I…"

"Of course that's what happened," Leo said with a snicker. "Dude's got it clear on his face."

He blinked. He needed to get this train back on the tracks and not circling him with conversations he wasn't in the mood to have or gossip that wasn't in any way helpful.

"Can we not consider ways to talk that won't besmirch…"

"He said besmirch!" Abe. Dammit. "He absolutely said besmirch, which means…"

Batya nodded and he consigned them both to applesauce. "So when is she coming to dinner?"

"You've already fed her," he said, knowing the words were flimsy and…well…slightly ridiculous. "I mean…"

"Yeah no," said Abe. "Here is different from the love fest you had back there in my sukkah, and whatever you did to make a bris on Jacob's Briarwood house. This is real, true dinner. In Rivertown. Tuesday night, full group, *here* where she is expected to *participate* and eat."

And technically really meet the people whom he considered family. But she wasn't ready for this group at full throttle. "No. Not happening."

Leo raised an eyebrow. "I directed cars in a vest that looks like a highlighter so that you could have your love fest, not to mention the fist fight I almost got into with Frank Maricelli in the middle of Briarwood. My reputation deserves protection, which means *the very least* you can do is get her to one of these."

And having clearly no other choice, considering once Leo got a hold of something, the man wouldn't stop, Artur nodded.

"Okay. I'll see what her schedule looks like."

THAT NIGHT, LIV and Artur were going over the projected list of story times and readers for the dreidl stage. But other information was spinning around in her head.

Was it too early to ask him to Shabbat dinner?

"You're distracted," he said, looking into her eyes. "What's going on?"

The way he was looking at her made her think he had something on his mind. "I could say the same."

He sighed, took a long drink from his glass. "I guess I have a question?"

She nodded. "Go ahead," she asked. "Ask me."

She watched the emotions play across his face, watched the storm gather. What did he want to know?

"Do you want to…go to a Tuesday night dinner at

Abe's?"

His question was deceptively light but she knew how important it was; talking with Anna at the planning meeting was beneficial in that regard. This was as important as a family dinner. "Sure," she said with a grin.

"Just like that?"

She nodded. "Just like that. It's important to you."

The smile on his face was perfect. "But you wanted to ask me something?"

"Yeah," she said. The goal was to keep it cool, make it easy. "I take it it's not too early for you to consider Shabbat dinner at my parents' place?"

He laughed, but the laugh was nervous. "Uh, maybe I..."

"No," she said, realizing she'd asked too much of him at this point in their...understanding of each other. "It's fine. I'll tell them you're too busy, and then kill my cousins."

"Your cousins?"

"Could be Leah, who was at last night's event with her boyfriend."

"The agent and the guy who's running the dreidl giveaway?"

"That's them," she said with a smile.

"Plausible," he said. "But not who I'd put my money on spilling the beans."

She laughed; this was the fixer doing his best to calm the situation And the fact she knew him well enough to know his moods at this point…

"You think it's Judith? She was also at last night's event with her fiancé?"

"Judith works with Jacob at Mitzvah Alliance, right?"

Liv nodded. "That's the one."

"Her fiancé is the most plausible culprit," he said with a smile that warmed her toes. "So…you…want to do these things or…?"

Aaaah. She realized Artur defaulted to the impartial fixer when he was nervous. She nodded, both to his question and then to her deduction. "Yes," she said. She grinned at him. "I guess we could call it a launch?"

He closed his eyes for a moment before leaning toward her. This time she caught his lips with hers, not pausing to talk, not pausing to analyze even as he probably wanted to. She'd analyzed enough.

All she wanted now was her reward.

Chapter Twenty-Three

F OR ARTUR, THINGS were getting what he considered…tangible.

The cycle of events were getting clearer, on schedules and timelines starting in two weeks. And as for his life? He was going to Liv's parents for Shabbat dinner the next Friday, after she came to Abe's on Tuesday.

Which meant he was making plans and ideas and wondering about going to go visit the garage. His car needed cleaning and this was about the only time he was going to have. Abe had grinned at him when he mentioned it.

But not just a normal grin; the 'there's something you're missing' grin. "Spill it," he said.

Amidst breakfast dishes and coffee cups, Abe made his proclamation. "You know, you should really think about taking her for a drive."

He gasped, almost dropping his coffee mug.

"I mean seriously," his best friend pointed out. "If this woman matters to you, then you're going to have to eventually tell her about your car and maybe let her inside."

"But I…never."

"Never doesn't matter when you've got someone like her. Remember. This isn't something I care too much about, but you do. And she will."

"Why would she care?"

"Because she cares about you, you ridiculous pinochle," said Batya from the other room as she came to join them. "I care about his smoking and his sauces. She'll care about your car and taking a drive with you."

Looking from Abe to Batya reminded him that they might know something about relationships and how important it was to build strong foundations with truth and not secrets.

"Okay," he said. "You're right. I'll call her."

In an hour he was in front of her house, glad she was free on this Saturday morning. "You ready?"

She nodded. "I am."

Of course, there was traffic. "We're driving to the city to go for a drive?"

He nodded. "I have…another car," he said. "This is…my usual day-to-day car. The car we're going to take a drive in is…my stress relief. It's… I've always been interested in cars as a hobby. Driving, going places. For whatever reason."

"Okay?"

"Anyway," he continued, "when they sold the Rivertown house, my parents gave me part of the money because of a birthday or whatever. Something. I got this one…the one that's waiting for us, I mean, when I got back to the States after the project I was doing."

She nodded, sat back against the seat as if she was going to analyze what he'd said and make it part of her own thoughts. "Okay," she said finally, making him nervous.

When they finally pulled into the owner spot in the climate-controlled garage, next to the vehicle under cover, his heart got stuck in his throat.

"You ready?" she asked.

He could clearly see the concern on her face. And he knew he definitely wasn't ready.

And yet if he continued to wait, he didn't think he'd ever *be ready.*

But for Liv? For the sake of what they were building? He'd try.

He opened the driver's side door, and motioned for her to follow him out of the car.

"Wait here," he said.

She nodded. "I'll be ready."

He took a deep breath, headed over to the cover and removed it, carefully, easily, waiting as she watched him.

And when it was finally off, he turned in her direction.

"This…"

He didn't know what she expected; the German sportscar sat gleaming before them, the sun coming through a window, setting off the beautifully polished paint job.

"As I told you, it's my stress relief," he said, stopping her from saying anything else. "I don't…let anybody in. At all. Not even my best friend."

He could see the disbelief run across her face before she tamped it down. "I'm…wow."

"Impressed? Mortified? Disgusted? Excited?"

"Not disgusted or mortified, that's for sure," she said, the words coming slowly as if she'd gathered them out of the ether when she needed them. "But I think the best way to think about it is that I'm…surprised. But yet not surprised."

She surprised the ever-loving crap out of him on a semi-regular basis. This was yet another one of those times.

"What…where did that come from?" he asked. "I mean why…?"

"I always drive," she said. "I mean us."

Which is something he thought about; if they were going somewhere together, she drove, otherwise he met her. "Which is true."

"And that's not to say I have a problem driving," she continued. "Honestly, I don't mind it at all."

And yet it sounded like she wasn't done talking; the sentence wasn't done. "But?"

"That's the thing that I couldn't put a finger on. You've never struck me as the type who doesn't…like driving, even though I understand the times when you say you don't drive because you're not familiar with the area and I am. Which meant there was something there."

He looked at her, stepped toward her as if drawn by a

force outside of his control. "I need to kiss you," he said.

"Go right ahead," she said. "My lips are…"

And he cut her off, his lips finding hers, his hands, his mouth, showing her how important this moment was to him. When he broke the kiss, he didn't waste time, buffing the car exterior quickly and preparing for a drive.

"Let's go," he said. And quicker than he'd expected, she was in his car. In the passenger seat, looking like she belonged there.

Which she did.

Which was still awkward to him, even though it wasn't bad. Instead, it was an awkward he looked forward to getting used to.

ARTUR HAD A *car*.

A ridiculously expensive sports car that he kept in a climate-controlled garage. Which he washed as stress relief. The leather she sat in was butter-soft, and the whole thing felt like a dream.

The man had layers, and instead of these layers putting Liv off, they pulled her in.

"Ask me anything," he invited as he drove toward the west side highway.

And that was the statement he made when she couldn't see his face? Did he want to hide his thoughts and expressions?

But there were many things she wanted to know about him. So many holes she wanted to fill.

But she went for the easiest one.

"How did you get into what you do?"

He took a deep breath as he drove, the fast car flying down the streets of New York. "Friend of mine from college had a relationship end. I don't remember the details anymore. But there weren't bad feelings on either side. He continued to live his life, you know. Doing what he does."

She didn't want to interrupt to ask what his friend did; from the way it sounded, the friend was some kind of creative.

"Well," he continued, "it turned out that wasn't the end of things. Because everybody who spoke to his ex, would ask questions about the end of the relationship and about him. They painted her as unserious, using him as the latest example of how she was a serial dater."

Yep. She got the hint that this was probably something she was supposed to know about. But the pressure, the situation made sense, for many reasons. Partially because it was her worst nightmare. But she wasn't telling him that. Instead the situation required something else.

"Ughhh. I hate that. I hate that the world is like that. So what happened?"

"My friend hated it too," he said. "Drove him absolutely nuts. He wanted to do something about it, but wasn't sure what to do and didn't want her to think he was trying to get attention off the end of the relationship. His goal, once he organized himself, was to take the heat off of her."

Which was a noble thought. Not many people would have thought like that.

"So," she asked, having organized herself again, "he called you?"

He nodded as they continued on their journey. "He just called me to talk, but he and I ended up working out a plan, and his team followed our script."

He hummed something, and she wasn't sure what it was. But he continued humming.

Clearly he wanted her to figure out the song... Images came to mind; a melody on an acoustic guitar.

And a music video opening with guy sitting behind a curtain watching a television. If she remembered correctly, the TV showed a young woman who was trying to escape a maze, covered in newspapers and stickers saying 'serial dater' in red letters. She was being yelled at with every step she took.

And the song started playing in her mind:

I could hide behind the curtains, let the world go on without
But then your path is tempest tossed,
full of thorns you don't deserve.
I know...the world does not make sense.
So I will take a step; step out into the world and

Be the one they talk to
instead of talk about.
I'll make sure that they know…you're the one for someone
even though you've never been for me.
I will take the heat and clean up all the thorns
because I've got a shield, a sword and a decent pair of shoes.
So you can be the good girl; I will be the bad boy.

Of course.

"Bad boy." By Chaim Marcus.

His first big solo single.

Naomi had been a huge fan of Zack Weisler's and Chaim's around the time of the beginning of their careers, and her sister had spent hours telling her about how much she loved Chaim for standing between his famous ex, Christi Quick, and the press.

Which meant that she knew the whole story behind the song, and the fact that Chaim Marcus's actions had quashed the conversation about his relationship with his ex, and let her be.

No ex of Christi Quick's since Chaim had done it; whether it was about her or about Chaim himself, who knew. But it stuck in her head.

"Yep," Artur said, breaking into her train of thought and confirming it without even saying anything. "Whatever you're thinking, you're right. Because the plan turned out to be impressive enough so people behind the scenes who knew about all of this asked whose idea it was, or more specifically who had directed the whole thing. My friend spoke up, said it was me. Not long after, I got offered a job by my friend's record label. And considering I enjoyed the process and the chase of the perfect solution, I took it."

She nodded. "So," she asked, still unfamiliar with the boundaries of his career. "Do you work with personal scandals?"

"Mostly corporate messes," he said as he drove them around a curve. "I'm not a political fixer. I'm not someone who's going to examine skeletons in people's closets or governmental secrets. It's my job to tell the PR people how to do their job after they messed up."

Which made sense, going back to why they met in the first place. "You," she said with a smile, "are an interesting guy. And I'm very lucky I know you."

The smile on his face was priceless, and she couldn't wait to kiss it off of him.

Chapter Twenty-Four

ARTUR HAD CONSULTED Abe and Sarah and Asher, who apologized after admitting that he might have been the one who tipped off Liv's aunt. Which meant he was as prepared as possible to attend Shabbat dinner with Liv and her parents.

Liv, however, was more nervous than he'd ever seen her; hiding her vulnerability behind her bravado, shaking only when he stopped holding her hand. Which meant that Artur found himself attempting to reassure her. "It's going to be fine," he said. "We're fine."

"And Naomi's going to be there to take off the heat."

Why it was necessary her sister was going to be there, he wasn't sure. But he wasn't going to say that to Liv when she was holding on to the idea for dear life, repeating the phrase as if it was a butterscotch candy she was sucking on.

"Either way," he continued, the fifth time they'd had that conversation and she'd had that response. "I've got really good babka, and I'm ready for anything."

Liv raised an eyebrow. "If anybody else had said that," she said, "I'd tell them they were full of pudding."

"But I'm not," he replied which seemed to relax her. "I promise we'll be fine." He paused and then looked up at her. "If you want me to drive, I will."

Which was enough to shock her into some degree of calm. "Are you sure?"

He nodded. "Look," he said. "If I drive, you'll concentrate on giving me directions and not on dinner."

The smile on her face was enough to keep him going. "Yes," he said. Okay. "We'll be good. No matter what."

And soon after, he pulled out of the guest space in front of Liv's town house, and then out of the development where the town house was.

"Where are we going?" he asked.

"Right." She shook her head, and there was that vulnerability again, the clear personal worry that she didn't want to show anybody else. "I'm just worried, but if Naomi doesn't come, I'll have to deal with my parents without family interference."

"We'll be fine no matter what," he said as he turned where she indicated he should. "What exactly makes you think she's not coming?"

"I would have heard from her by now if she was," Liv replied. "I haven't heard from her at all since the party. And I'm concerned that she's avoiding me…because she's not coming."

He blinked. Abe's backyard barbecue pop-up had been a few weeks before. "Is it usual for the two of you not to be in contact for that long a period?"

"It is, unless there's something going on, like my cousin's wedding prep and dinner."

He nodded. "Brace yourself either way," he said. "I'm with you every step of the way."

"Which is why I'm still sitting here and not running to find and strangle my sister."

He smiled, her hand on top of his for a brief moment as it came off the gear shift. "We're going to be fine," he said. "I promise."

And no matter what happened, he'd do his best to make sure that what he told her was true.

OF COURSE LIV'S phone buzzed with a message from Naomi just after they'd greeted her parents.

She squeezed Artur's shoulder.

"Drank too much water before getting in the car," she said as she made her quick escape, jamming a button on her phone to call her sister as she closed the bathroom door.

"Hello?"

"I very much…hate you," Liv said as she walked into the bathroom. Which was the best place for privacy.

"Why?" Naomi asked.

Of course she wasn't there. She'd expected it, felt the tell-tale signs of her sister's attempt to avoid her, her parents and whatever drama she might have been expecting.

But telling Naomi she knew what was up her bag of tricks was not something Liv felt like disclosing, or something that would make her yell. Instead, she kept it simple. "Because you're not here for dinner tonight."

"You miss Shabbats all the time," Naomi said. "Life was nuts. I'm home; you're there."

"But this is different, Naomi," Liv said. "Which you would have known if you, you know, made an attempt to call me?"

Her sister's dramatic sigh reminded her of a wind gust. "What exactly is so different about this night as opposed to the…however many other non-holiday Shabbats?"

"Right," she said. "Okay." But she needed to be calm, cool, collected and ready. "So this time, tonight, Artur's here."

She heard what could have been the sound of the phone dropping or a glass breaking or something.; she wasn't sure which one it was or why…

And yet.

When Naomi came back to the phone, she was breathing heavily. "He's at Shabbat dinner for why?"

"Because Mom called me and was asking about him, like they were the gossip treasurers of Briarwood synagogue or something."

"I don't get it," Naomi said. "This makes absolutely no sense whatsoever. Like… You're…just getting to know this guy and she's ASKING you about him."

"Well," she said. "I know. But I felt like it made sense for me to ask him. And he wanted to come, because it means something to me. He actually is prepared to swing a proverbial sword on my behalf tonight because you're not here."

"We're not…this is ridiculous," Naomi said, clearly unable to find words that made sense. "You don't deserve that, just because two people saw you two in public."

The bathroom was smothering, if not sweltering, and Naomi clearly didn't understand their parents' actions. Of course she didn't; her sister was somewhere, doing something that kept her away. Not here.

When Liv needed her, not just for company or help but to understand.

Clearly that wasn't happening, which meant Liv had to get through to her sister using the only…weapon she had. Her words.

"You," Liv managed, "if you spend time with a guy, people can say it's casual and be okay with it. But me? I spend time with someone, everybody watches me. Everybody thinks it's suddenly a big deal. So he came. And I owe him for this…"

"You don't owe him. If a guy really likes you, if he's special," her sister said, "he'd do something for you. He'd help you. He'd offer his sword."

"Okay," Liv said. Desperately trying not to read into what Naomi said regarding Jason, who seemed to be noticeably absent from Naomi's discourse and existence. "But anyway, none of it matters," she said, "because he's here. And you're not."

"I'm sorry," Naomi said. "Really."

"We'll talk at some point," Liv managed, the tone that had come into her lexicon of 'it's fine but not really.'

"I owe you," Naomi said.

"Yes, you do," Liv replied, as she ended the call.

Thankfully, when she opened the door to the bathroom, her parents had headed off and Artur was waiting with a hanger, talking to her mother through the hallway. Without a word, the lovely man took her coat, hung it up and put it away before putting his arms around her.

"I told you," he whispered, his voice making her insides jelly, "you have my sword."

"Hopefully you don't need it," she replied as she headed into the kitchen.

DESPITE LIV'S CONCERNS, the night and the dinner had gone pretty well; the candlesticks that were Liv's mother's prized possessions reminded him of candlesticks he'd seen pretty much every Friday night during his childhood.

"So where were you bar mitzvahed again?" Liv's father asked.

"Rivertown Hebrew," he said.

The gentleman, who cut a good London broil, nodded. "Good to hear. Now where do you work again?"

He smiled. "I worked in-house for a company for a while, then I moved to a consulting firm for quite a number of years," he said. "But I had burnout and ended up doing five years working on a Mitzvah Alliance project in Eastern Europe."

Liv's mother made a noise that sounded like approval.

"And now?" Liv's father asked, continuing what Artur now was absolutely sure was some kind of interrogation.

But he was prepared; as Asher had explained both at Jacob's house and over a hastily conducted conversation in between talking about Jewish players and the Empires, this was the first time Liv had ever brought someone to her parent's house, and apparently, from what he'd heard from Asher, the first time the family noticed she'd actually noticed anybody.

Hence the full court press from Liv's parents. Of course, he never minded answering questions.

"Now? I'm back," he said, smiling as if there wasn't any other thing he'd rather do than be there with her or them on this Friday night. Because there wasn't. Shabbas dinner was warm and comfortable. If he could help make Liv feel any of those things on a night where her natural inclination was to feel the complete opposite, he'd submit to any kind of interrogation possible. Including interrogation by applesauce.

But talking about his professional goals in a way that made him look stable to concerned parents?

Easy.

"At the moment," he said, "I'm working for the Empires on a temporary basis here in Briarwood. While I'm doing that, I'm investigating a few possibilities for my next gig, one of which is with the Empires."

He saw her smile; found himself very glad he'd told her already about what his plans were.

Liv reached for his hand, "I think he might be talking about possibly doing something with one of Leah's clients."

He nodded, taking her hand in his. "I think that's what it is. They haven't told me very much. Odds are, they won't until the end of the opening here."

"But," Liv's father said. "Regardless of what position you end up taking, you're going to stay in the New York area?"

He nodded, taking a bite of his challah. G-d that was good. "My expertise is in fixing large-scale corporate PR crises. I have experience in other crisis forms, but that's where I'm comfortable working. Most of the companies that usually hire someone like me tend to be based in the New York area. But I'm actually hoping to go in-house."

"Freelance, or having your own shop has the whole time dilemma, right?" her mother said. "You set your own schedule, but you have to be more active in finding things."

He nodded, smiling. "I'll always have the potential of getting the 3 a.m. phone call, because corporate crises wait for nobody, but the reality is that if I'm in-house, I might be able to see that coming and work with the company to avoid the danger."

"So," Liv interjected, "if you were in-house with the Empires before this…"

"There is a good possibility I would have jumped in and never let Flaire's plan see the light of day."

"Well," Liv's mother said, smiling at her older daughter, "then it's a good thing he didn't have to see Flaire before she came to Briarwood."

He wasn't sure Liv would agree to that. "I'm glad I met you," he said to Liv. "But there were, and still are, a lot of people that were hurt."

And instead of glaring at him, she smiled. "Yeah. We definitely would have met in other circumstances for sure. I wouldn't wish the pain Briarwood residents have been dealing with on anybody."

He squeezed her hand. And sitting there, right then, he knew he wasn't going to let her go.

Chapter Twenty-Five

T HE MORNING AFTER Shabbat dinner was supposed to be relaxing; Liv had very loose plans to meet Artur to inspect the vendor area in the afternoon and have dinner and maybe go for some kind of drive.

Even the chamber of commerce members were thrilled with the way everything was going; she had been lazily checking social media only to see a new email to come in to her inbox. When she clicked on it, she saw that it was an invitation to a Champagne toast celebrating the dreidl once it was installed.

Things were coming together, and it felt really good.

But all that lazy excitement went out the window when she saw there was an incoming call from Judith.

"What are your plans for the afternoon?" Judith asked innocently.

She raised an eyebrow. "To relax, have a nice day, maybe inspect the vendor area now that it's been constructed. Why?"

"Because," Judith said with an extended sigh, "I've been informed that there's a problem with the bridesmaids dresses we picked."

"And," Liv wondered, "what problem is that?"

"They were retired by the designer, which means we have to pick new ones. As soon as possible. We have an appointment at the dress shop this afternoon."

Of course she did.

The only person more efficient than she was had acted and now they had a new fitting date.

Of course, that meant she could be more specific about trying to determine who was responsible for spilling the beans to her parents. "Coincidentally enough," Liv replied, "I have a bone to pick with you, my dear cousin, about information."

"I see," she said. "Well, you can get some information at the shop. And then, at brunch."

And as she ended the call, she realized she needed to make another. "Hey," she said as Artur picked up the phone. "Gotta cancel on you today."

"What's up?"

"Bridesmaid dress disaster," she replied with a laugh. "I've got an appointment at a dress shop on the other side of the county."

"Need a ride?"

She laughed. There was something about Artur and his driving these days, as if now that she'd uncorked his abilities, he wanted to drive her everywhere. "You don't mind driving me across the county?"

"No," he said. "Gives me more time with you."

"And," she said, "if you drop me off, you can go work on your other car in the city while I hang out with my cousins."

"Do you want a ride back?"

"I think you just want a debrief."

"That too," he said with a laugh. "How about you send me a carrier pigeon when you're done and we'll figure that out."

"I like the sound of that plan."

Not long after she ended the call, she was on the other side of the county, sitting in Artur's car, grinning up at him. "You know," she said. "Long as I'm here I can try on dresses for the Hanukkah party."

"I cannot wait to see you in whatever you get."

She smiled at his excitement. "I think that deserves a kiss," she said.

"Your desire is my command," he replied.

She leaned in, found his lips with hers. She ran her hands through his hair and lost herself completely in the taste and feel of him.

When she broke the kiss and stepped out of the car, she waved back at him before heading toward the door of the shop.

She shook her head as Artur drove away. "Cannot believe I'm here today," she said.

"I can't believe that the dress I picked five months ago was retired by the designer, I mean who does that?"

STACEY AGDERN

Leah's long dramatic sigh made Liv feel better, and she hugged her.

"I do have a bone to pick with you," Liv said.

"Yes. Bones will be picked at brunch, according to my sister," Leah said, waving at Judith, who was standing in the doorframe of the shop to greet them.

"We're changing colors," Judith said with a grin as she ushered them inside. "So we're picking blue dresses."

Having received the orders, Liv looked through the dresses the saleswoman who'd been working with them had pulled. Her mission was to find a dress that would highlight her curves, not make her look like a blueberry.

"Why blue exactly?" Leah asked.

"It's a color that means a great deal to both of us," Judith said with a smile. "And if we have to change the color, we decided we might as well just have that one."

Which, as far as Liv was concerned, worked for her. It was a slog for sure, but once she found a few she liked, she pointed to them and asked for them in her size.

"Absolutely," the saleswoman said as she directed her into a fitting room.

Three dresses later, she'd ranked them and informed Judith of her choice.

"Great."

When she returned to the fitting room, she got the saleswoman's attention. "I also need a cocktail dress, for a holiday party I'm attending…"

"Yes," the saleswoman said excitedly. "I'll bring a few dresses that will look stunning on you."

As the saleswoman headed off, the door was kept open by a very familiar pair of fingers. Of course, Naomi was here.

"Yes?"

"I wasn't here long enough to miss the conversation about cocktail dresses. For the mentorship party?"

Liv glared at her sister. "I'm still mad at you."

"I understand. You deserve to be angry; I owe you. But the dress is for the mentorship party?"

"Yeah," Liv said. She turned to her sister. "I'll need makeup, okay?"

Naomi nodded. "Got it."

"And considering," Liv glared at Judith and Leah, as they sat at brunch after the dresses had been ordered and organized, "my mother called me and informed me that your mother had told her I was out with someone, someone needs to fess up."

"That." Judith said, shaking her head. "It wasn't Ash, because I told him he needed to keep his mouth shut around my mom."

Leah sighed. "I think it was Samuel because he got a random text from Isaac Lieberman when we were at my parents' for something on Sunday, and he asked me why Isaac was excited he met you...which meant story time. So that's on me."

Fascinating.

Apparently Artur had put his money on the wrong man. Either way, he would get a kick out of this one.

She couldn't wait to tell him.

ON THE DRIVE to Manhattan, Artur had gotten a call from Emily Gould-Smythe. "Just a heads-up," she said. "I'm hearing the sculpture is not holding for whatever reason. Which means it actually might not survive transport. And yes, our consultant has spoken to the sculptor about the power of fastening agents, but he is not listening. Which means you're going to have to fix this."

Artur nodded, thoughts running through his head.

The problem needed to be fixed from the bottom up.

"I'm going to have to get a consultant of my own on site immediately," he said. "As well as find a facility big enough to hold both the sculpture and the tools my consultant's going to need to pull everything together."

"Good. I like the fact you have a good bead on the situation. And remember."

Emily's warning didn't have to be articulated. This was becoming a larger problem, and he was coming up against that NDA.

Which meant he was going to have to find a solution for that…as well as the dreidl.

But would Liv understand? Could he create a situation

where the fragile trust they'd started to create would survive an NDA?

And that afternoon, when he listened to Liv as she talked about how important the event was going to be, as she told him how the political eyes were going to be on her as she moved from Briarwood Mayor to County Legislator representing a larger district, he hoped he could.

Chapter Twenty-Six

DINNER AT ABE'S had basically been a briefing/planning meeting for the kickoff party; he had been testing out recipes and Liv ate waaaay too much. Artur's friends were a hoot up close; she knew how lucky he was to have them. It was also fun to realize that both Ash and Samuel had spilled the beans about the relationship to her aunt and had both taken responsibility in different ways.

Naomi had done makeup for Liv, Leah, and Judith. In the dress she'd bought for the night, Liv felt like a queen.

And the party itself was gorgeous. The kids from the mentorship program mixed with members from the chamber of commerce, the temple sisterhood and the Empires; there were best-selling authors, sports agents, artists and heads of huge charity funds as well as members of the county legislature.

Liv was in her element.

And the auction was the hit of the night.

"And if you like these," Sarah, the Hanukkah planner, who had been convinced to act as auctioneer, yelled, "you're going to love the sculpture when it arrives this week."

As Liv stood and watched the festivities, finding pride in how much the auction was raising for the program, a few of her new colleagues in the county legislature came up to join her.

"I cannot wait to see the sculpture," said her new colleague who represented the district that included Hollowville. "I love seeing other communities celebrate their Jewish populations."

"The sports team angle is fascinating too," said the new colleague who represented a district that included Rivertown. "I love seeing local teams involve themselves in village events."

The caucus leader said, "And I am looking forward to chatting further with you. I'm really enjoying the way you see issues."

Liv felt like she was flying. "Thank you," she said.

"I'm absolutely looking forward to the impact you're going to make on county policy," Artur had said as they headed out to the car at the end of the evening.

And, she decided, she was looking forward to seeing the impact that he was going to make on her. As it was, with Artur by her side, she'd felt stronger, more confident. If she had to put a finger on why, she'd say that because he was so uniquely himself, she felt comfortable being herself.

And she couldn't wait to see what they would become together.

AFTER HE DROPPED Liv off, Artur paced his bedroom in Abe's place. He needed to find a location where he could get the sculpture fixed safely and carefully. He'd been putting this off for way too long and he needed to get started.

Not to mention, he desperately needed to find a way to get a message to Liv without telling her. He had to show her he trusted her.

He picked up his phone and went through his contacts, making notes, and a game plan. There were a bunch of calls he needed to make before the sculpture arrived and Hanukkah started in Briarwood.

The next morning, he left Abe's place, having arranged with Emily Gould-Smythe to borrow some office space in one of the buildings the Empires owned in Hollowville.

"I have to make a few calls," he'd said. "I need a space behind closed doors to arrange for the contingencies."

"Go ahead," she'd told him. "You have free rein of some empty offices."

Once he'd settled in the building, he got to work, the list he'd made in front of him. The first call he needed to make was to Jacob. "Do you mind if I crash at your place?"

His friend, the ridiculous man, laughed. "Which one?"

"Briarwood."

"Go right ahead," he said. "I've got this ridiculously massive house and way too many guest rooms for my own good.

That one's closer to the event, hmm?"

Artur nodded. "Yep. That's the only reason I'm asking you. That and you're the only person I know in Briarwood who might have access to the kind of space I might need."

"Really?" Jacob said, sounding intrigued. "Talk to me."

"Well," Artur replied, "I might need a private space where some kind of…repair can take place."

Jacob nodded. "Yep. I think the garage at the Briarwood house might do you some good. Repair of…?"

"A contingency plan," he said. "Don't want to speak it aloud because I don't want to speak it into existence."

"Yes. Superstitions. Okay. You've got access to any and all the things you'll need. The one I'm thinking of has a separate entrance. So do with it what you will."

"Thank you," Artur said. "Very much appreciated. Again. And I owe you."

"No, you don't. Those words make no sense coming out of your mouth. I know what's riding on this."

Artur did too. But he wasn't done with his calls. When he ended that call, he searched in his wallet for Sarah's card. She answered the phone right away. "Hello?"

"Hey, it's Artur" he said. "Listen. I need a favor."

"Sure," Sarah said. "You know me. Anything within reason."

"Great," Artur replied. "It's probably not that big. Because what I need is to talk to Isaac and I don't have his number."

"That's not big at all." And suddenly the phone sounded like it was moving, whispers in the background.

And then…

"Hello?"

"Isaac," he said. "This is…"

"Yes, Artur. Hello. Did you have a question for me?"

"Yes," Artur said, really glad he remembered. "I'm wondering how you feel about working with wooden pieces."

There was a long pause, where Artur felt he was going to be completely sunk. Except…

"I've actually been dabbling," Isaac said when he came back to the phone. "But it's not something I talk about much unless people want special wooden chuppah holders for their weddings. Why?"

"Would you be able to help reinforce a sculpture in the event that it's refusing to hold its shape?"

Once again, a long pause and Artur thought he was going to be sunk. "Wood?"

"Yep."

"I can't guarantee anything," Isaac finally said after what felt like the longest pause of the afternoon. "But sure. I'll take a crack at it if you need me to."

Which was the only thing he could hope for. Isaac was a brilliant sculptor, and his 'dabbling' was someone else's masterpiece. "Good," he said. "I think I'm going to. Let me get your number and I'll call you if I need to."

And as he ended the call, he was ready as he could be.

Chapter Twenty-Seven

THE NIGHT BEFORE the event's opening Liv spend hours in her office checking guest lists. The team, the board of legislators and other county officials, people from Hollowville and Rivertown, the sisterhood and a few other individuals.

The event schedule started in the evening and the sculpture was supposed to arrive the next morning. Of course she had a meeting with Mayor-Elect Fields-Kramer in the morning, the handing over the keys as it were.

Except she should be there when the sculpture arrived. It would feel wrong if she wasn't, so she should try to move the meeting.

When she made the suggestion to the mayor-elect, Liv was met with resistance.

"Can't," Terry Fields-Kramer said. "I had to somehow create time in my schedule to meet with you now."

And this time, it was the random buzzer she set but never ended up using that heralded the end of this meeting.

It didn't bode well.

The meeting had run late even though these meets never

do, and the sculpture had presumably already arrived. Artur was there and she trusted him…

But she wanted to be there. She should be there.

Liv couldn't push the new mayor out of her office fast enough, before she grabbed her coat and ran out the door, not even stopping to look at the clock.

Just outside the window on the bottom floor of town hall, she saw Artur, his back to her. Talking to…someone.

Where was the sculpture?

The person he was speaking to gestured as if he was doing some kind of magic, hands all over the place.

What was going on?

She had to get there. Liv burst out the door and headed toward Artur.

ARTUR WAS DEALING with a problem. He'd gotten Naomi's email at the party the night before, and he'd quickly dashed off a message, explaining the situation and what he needed from her.

He stared out the window, waiting for the sculpture to arrive, before running down to meet the truck, hoping Naomi would do what he needed her to.

Of course, when the sculpture arrived, the situation was as bad as Emily Gould-Smythe feared.

"It's in pieces," the sculptor confirmed.

THE DREIDL DISASTER

Not wanting to dwell or wait or create a situation where Liv would find herself here before she spoke to Naomi, "We'll take care of it from here," he said.

The sculptor headed off, presumably to get as far from the situation as possible, having already been informed by someone else from the Empires public relations team that the sculpture would be fixed without his involvement or input.

"Where is this going?" the driver asked.

Artur pulled out his phone and read off Jacob's address. "I'll meet you there and take you to the garage."

The driver nodded and got into the truck, pulling away into the winter air.

"Let him fix this quickly. Let this be fixable."

Having stated his hope aloud, he unlocked his car and was about to get in when he felt a hand on his shoulder. "What's going on?"

Liv.

The one time in the world he didn't want to see her, she was there.

Timing, luck, bad miracles and all of that.

But timing was timing and whatever was going to happen was going to happen. Pulling himself together, he looked up at her, hoping she'd understand him. "I have to go take care of something right now. I'll call you later, okay?"

The woman was too perceptive for her own good, looking up at him as if she could decipher something from the expression on his face. Hopefully she couldn't manage it.

"You have a problem?" she asked. "Can I help?" Liv's eyes were wide, inquisitive and gorgeous, and what he really wanted was to tell everybody to go to Hades and bring her back to the office for a private meeting. But he couldn't.

And he couldn't tell her why either.

"No," he said. "I've got this under control."

"You have it under control," she repeated, in that way of hers that revealed she knew more than he was telling her. "This was something you planned for."

Finding absolutely nothing wrong with her statement, he nodded. "I plan for pretty much all contingencies," he said. "It's my job. Speaking of which, I need to go. I'll call you later?"

"No," she said, her entire expression and body language a stop sign.

Applesauce.

Dammit.

"What contingency are you fixing?"

He loved how perceptive she was, loved how brilliant and wonderful she was and yet in that moment he hated it.

"I can't tell you," he said, as clearly and as slowly as he could. "Call Naomi, or she's going to call you. Listen to her." And then he looked at her, hoping she'd understand. "Please?"

She didn't nod, just looked at him. "Why?" she asked, her voice daggers. "Why won't you tell me yourself? What's going on?"

"I can't tell you," he said. "Trust me. Please?"

"Like you trusted me enough to keep me aware of a possibility that something could go wrong with this situation? And not just an in the air possibility...a possibility that you planned to be an actual thing?"

For just one moment he held his breath, hoping she'd get it. Hoping that she could decipher what he was saying.

She shook her head, and in her expression, every single hope he'd had winked out like a set of bad electric lights. "I think not."

And as she headed off, the worst thing was that he couldn't follow her.

Not only was he prevented by the NDA from explaining the situation, but also and more importantly, he couldn't wait. He had to get to Jacob's house before the mess arrived, and make the necessary arrangements so that it would become a sculpture. All of this was on his shoulders, and he couldn't take the time to go make sure she understood how much she meant to him.

His heart pounded.

She was pissed and he couldn't explain himself.

He couldn't tell her.

He needed a miracle.

For her, so that he could explain himself and not lose the woman who was becoming more important to him than breathing.

But also for the town and everybody who'd been waiting

for this celebration and deserved so much more than a broken dreidl.

LIV DIDN'T WATCH Artur's car as he drove away; she'd turned away, and didn't look for the familiar blue paint job in the distance. But she didn't move either; she stood on the corner until she was capable of moving, assured that he was gone.

Her heart started to pound against her chest, and of course, that was when the snow started to fall. Of course.

Miracle of miracles.

Not.

She couldn't cry. Couldn't break down. Instead, she called Judith.

Judith answered the phone quickly. "Hi, Liv."

"Good time? Are you in the middle of something?"

"Where are you?" Judith said. "Why are you calling me now? Is everything okay?"

"No," Liv said. "Nothing is okay. I want ice cream and some of the soofganiyot the Cupcake Stop is making for the food court at the installation and all the things I shouldn't have. But I can't have any of those things."

"You need to calm down," Judith said. "Can you come to the building?"

The building, where Asher and the Mitzvah Alliance, aka

Artur's friend Jacob, rented space in the business improvement district. Where they'd met only a few weeks before, planning the party they'd had only days before.

Which would mean walking in front of people, past spaces that were preparing for the evening's festivities and the beginning of Hanukkah. And the legacy of hers that would fall to pieces, leaving her looking ridiculous in front of new colleagues and old friends.

She couldn't put on a mask, couldn't look like everything was fine. Not there.

"No," she replied. "I don't."

Of course, Naomi was beeping on the other line. She was the last person Liv wanted to talk to in the mood she was in. Whether it was petty, painful, upset, Liv couldn't face the fact that Artur seemed to trust her sister with important information when he didn't trust her.

Which sounded awful, but that was what the situation was.

"I just…"

"Go get chocolate," Judith said, the reason she'd called her cousin coming clearly into focus. Her cousin was smart and understood enough about her and the situation to give her advice she couldn't rationalize herself. "Go take a breather and then call me when you're sitting down and out of the…snow that's falling outside my window."

She ended the call, knowing that if she stayed on the phone any longer, she would get comfortable enough to break down. And that was the one thing she couldn't do. She followed Judith's advice and headed toward Stars and Icing. If a gelt latte couldn't help her this Hanukkah, nothing could.

Because after she swallowed down the mix of caffeine and chocolate, she still had a job to do. People to impress.

A life to lead. A legacy to fix.

She'd break down later, in her bedroom with the door closed.

ARTUR CALLED JACOB from the car. "The mess is on its way, and I'm coming with it."

"I got this," his friend said. "You just concentrate on getting here and not wrecking in this weather."

"Thank you," he said. "I owe you."

"Nope. You don't. Just get here safe."

Of course, Jacob was waiting outside when he got in, directing him up toward the garage he'd parked his cars in. "Good," Jacob said. "This way."

Artur followed his friend through the hallway toward the second garage space.

"This should work, right?"

Artur nodded as Jacob opened the door. Tools were all set up on a workbench. The dreidl, or at least the box containing the pieces of the dreidl, was on the center of the floor.

"This will work." It had to.

But he didn't think about alternatives now; he began to pace the length of the workbench as he waited for help to arrive.

"I don't know who you called," Jacob said, "but they'll be here."

"Don't know what the roads are like," Artur said. "Westchester County roads are inconsistent, especially on route nine in Rivertown, and I'm not sure how well Abe drives in snow."

Because Abe had volunteered to pick Isaac up in Hollowville on the way to Briarwood.

That was friendship, Artur knew.

"You want me to go and get him?"

"Uh…"

"I've got a thing in the other garage," Jacob continued, in a tone that meant he was serious. "So, I could."

"I'm guessing," Artur replied with a laugh, "that your thing is large and weird and British?"

"You'd be right," Jacob said. "And horrifying, if I say myself, but it works in snow."

Artur shook his head. "No. It's not just Abe who's coming," he clarified. "You probably don't want to drive Isaac in save-the-day mode."

"Last time I drove him anywhere was to the latke fry-off," he replied. "Ixnay on the driving *period* with him after that."

Artur shuddered. "That must have been an experience. I only caught the arrival. So."

"What do you mean by 'save-the-day mode'?"

Right. Artur hadn't been this loose with his tongue around Jacob before. Which meant he needed to translate. "Isaac is coming to fix the dreidl and Abe is driving him."

"That I know. But what about Isaac's being in some kind of…mode?"

"The longer he seems to mull the idea of fixing the dreidl, the more convinced he becomes that it's fated and that he can make a miracle out of this whole," he waved his hand, "fakakta disaster."

Jacob nodded as the translation did what it was supposed to. Because apparently he was only comprehensible in this box of cool collected ass with a sword for Jacob.

Boxes. He hated being put into boxes. Despised it.

And that was exactly what he did to Liv. He could have taken other ways to make this better, but he didn't.

He threw his head back, sighed, and hoped he could figure out how to fix things with Liv.

Chapter Twenty-Eight

THE BENEFIT OF Stars and Icing over Cupcake Stop was that on most days, behind a Stars and Icing countertop wasn't someone who wanted to talk Liv's ear off.

People were pleasant, of course, but there was a motion about Stars and Icing. People were there for a reason and then went. As opposed to Cupcake Stop where people literally stopped.

Which meant it was a rare joy for her to sit down by the window in Stars and Icing and not talk to a soul.

"Liv," Naomi's voice out of nowhere. "Get over here."

Of course her sister would interrupt her private time with her gelt latte. Of course she would. She still wasn't ready to or interested in talking to anybody, let alone her sister. "I...what?"

"We need to talk. Now."

Liv blinked. "No, we don't."

"I need to talk to you about something." Naomi paused, and Liv wondered what the hell her sister was doing.

"More specifically I have something for you."

"Now is not the time," Liv said, brandishing her coffee

in her sister's direction. "You need to leave."

"Not leaving until you talk to me."

Liv threw her head back, powered by the sigh that could end all sighs. "What could be so important that you are this insistent," she managed while glaring at her sister.

"There's something someone else told me," she said, biting her lip.

Was Naomi nervous?

"Anyway, you really need to know what it is."

Liv blinked. "What?"

"I have a message for you from Artur."

And if nothing could switch the mood of the moment and of the room completely, it would be those words and that name.

Naomi pulling a sentence with those words and that name was the very last thing Liv wanted, or for that matter, needed. "No. That is the LAST name I need to hear right now."

"You need to hear this and I'm not leaving until you do."

"Excuse me?"

Naomi looked around and gestured to the crowd of people starting to enter the shop. "If you want to make a scene," her sister said, "fine. I'll make a scene. But I suspect you don't."

Temporary moment of dealing with betrayal and heartbreak over, Liv desperately needed to get back to life, caffeine, and her job. Not to listen to the insanity that her sister felt like she needed to deliver. "I have to go, Naomi. This isn't a good time."

"Fine. I'll head to the office with you," Naomi said. "We need privacy anyway."

And in that moment, Liv saw the determination in her sister's expression. Liv knew that expression, it meant Naomi wouldn't take no for an answer; the version of her sister who was stubborn and inescapable and tenacious. Naomi was not budging.

"Fine," Liv said, "but you need to be quick."

Bargain made, Liv followed her sister to the town hall building, not knowing what she was getting into.

OUT OF NOWHERE, the door to Jacob's garage flew open, revealing Isaac, with his best friend close behind.

"Move away," Isaac said. "And let me work."

Artur pointed toward the box. "This is what you've got to work with."

"And what do you want me to make out of this—" Isaac gestured widely toward the box "—whatever this is?"

"A dreidl."

If Isaac had any misgivings, he didn't show them. Which was encouraging...maybe.

"Let me know if there's anything you need," Jacob added. "Tools, materials."

Isaac shook his head, glancing around at the saws and the fasteners that sat on the work bench Jacob had brought in to the garage. "This should be it."

And as Isaac went to work, Artur started to pace.

LIV LEAD NAOMI into town hall and closed the door to her office behind them.

"So," she said, looking at her sister from behind her desk. "You said you have to tell me something. Talk."

"I do," Naomi said. "I have a message for you from Artur."

"You said," Liv told her sister. "And I'm angry with him right now, because he couldn't tell me what was going on, which means he doesn't trust me. And we're done. So unless what you have to say is relevant to information I need to make sure this event goes without a hitch, I don't want to hear it."

"Artur didn't tell you because he was given instructions not to, by his boss," she said, as if it was the easiest bit of information in the world to figure out. "But because he knew you needed to know, he tried to circumvent it by telling someone who had nothing to do with the team or the celebration."

And that was interesting, surprising even.

That he'd gone to that distance, even confided in someone who was still on shaky ground with her, to ensure she got the information, was astounding.

And a level of trust she hadn't anticipated in her upset haze.

"Whoa."

"Yep." Naomi nodded, looking slightly vindicated. "That's why I called you, but because you ignored my call and didn't call me back, you didn't know what was going on."

"I was upset at him and took it out on the fact that he told me to call you," she said. "But okay. So he chose to tell you what was going on in order to circumvent the NDA. What did he tell you?"

"Now we're cooking," Naomi replied, grinning like an LED. "His boss told him not to tell you that the sculpture had arrived damaged. And when he's working a job like he is, when a company figure slaps an NDA on some kind of policy, even something that isn't officially one, his hands are tied."

"Which is great, but then I need to know these things. It's important, I mean..."

"Which is why," Naomi said, "stay with me here...there's a reason we're talking now."

Liv nodded, swallowing back...something.

"Anyway," Naomi continued, "the man engineered a way for you to find out something when he couldn't tell you himself. Now I don't know what you think of that or him, but the fact he trusted you enough to try and circumvent a situation when his hands were tied? Should tell you a lot more."

Which made the conversation with Artur that she'd had much clearer. Much more understandable.

It wasn't *I don't want to tell you.* It was *I can't tell you.*

Emphasis on the *can't.*

Now much more aware of what was going on and what she was going to be told, she asked, "What's going on now?"

Naomi tapped her fingers against the table. "My guess is that he's with the dreidl, attempting to fix it."

"And what should I do?"

"Act as if you don't know a thing and decide what you are going to do when you see him."

She had a lot to do and decisions to make.

ARTUR FOLLOWED ABE and Jacob out of the garage/workspace into an entertainment area; couches and large televisions dotted the walls of this room just inside the house.

"So?"

Abe and Jacob were both staring at him as he sat down. "Nu? What is this? Is this an intervention, an interrogation, or both?"

"You're a mess," Abe said, neither confirming nor denying. "You're pacing and you're making Isaac nervous."

Which was true, he realized as he fought the impulse to stand and pace across the carpeting.

"Don't," Jacob added with a laugh. "You're making me dizzy. So what's going on?"

Knowing the both of them, he realized that he needed to fess up, which meant he told the story from the beginning.

And what he hoped was going on.

"What's more important?" Abe asked once Artur finished. "The woman or the job?"

Artur raised an eyebrow. "Non-disclosure…has nothing to do with what I feel is important or not. It's not my information to play with."

"Exactly," Jacob said. "Good answer."

Except from his tone, Artur could tell that there was something more coming. "But what?"

Jacob nodded. "I think the bigger problem is not about how you didn't tell her, but that you didn't explain that in your line of work, there are sometimes situations where you *can't* tell her what's going on, and that in those times, she needs to trust you to know when and how to get her information she needs."

He nodded. And that made sense, letting him feel that there was a chance, a possible chance to help Liv understand…and fix the argument they'd had.

Now, he had to wait for sundown and the biggest Hanukkah miracle he'd ever hoped for.

Chapter Twenty-Nine

ISAAC PULLED OFF a miracle, and the dreidl was delivered to the space in the center of town where they'd built the stage.

The speakers were wonderful, talking about unity and inclusion. Even the members of the JHPA who brought a menorah and candles did a wonderful job, and the entire crowd said the blessings.

But the thing that burned the brightest? Liv's smile.

She was effervescent; she was gorgeous. And the entire crowd was so happy.

The calendar of events would start the next day, and everything that happened was a testament to her and the work she'd done.

He needed to go and find her.

"Go get her," Abe said with a grin. "Go find the girl."

Following his best friend's smart advice, he headed toward a spot she could see from the stage…

"Artur," a woman he recognized as his boss, Emily, said, "I'd like to talk to you if you have the time."

And almost miraculously he met Liv's eye…as she

winked and turned away.

"If now isn't a good time," Emily started. "I actually have a proposition for you."

"Now is good," he said. "I'm interested."

"We're about to make history and we'd like you on board to help."

"History?"

Emily nodded and beckoned over one of the player reps who'd lit the candles. "Artur Rabinovitch, this is Carly Emerson. Our backup goaltender for this coming season."

"Nice to meet you," she said.

And as they continued to talk, all Artur could think about was how excited he was to tell Liv.

AFTER THE DREIDL was unveiled and the candles were lit, Liv found herself in the middle of many conversations, but none of them the one she really wanted to have.

With Artur.

As she finished up her business and headed toward the food vendor section, she felt a hand on her shoulder.

"If you're indulging yourself, I'd like some, too."

She turned around and met his eyes with hers. "I'm sorry."

"I'm sorry."

From the expression on his face, it felt like his words had

intertwined with hers. "Can I go first?"

He nodded. "Yes," he said. "I will always listen to you no matter what you need to say."

"I'm sorry for presuming. I'm sorry for not listening to you and taking the fact you couldn't tell me what was going on personally, and I'm sorry for not understanding," she managed.

"I'm sorry I didn't give you the right words…"

She looked up at him. "I'm intrigued, but you have to explain."

"I should have let you know that in my line of work, there are things that might sometimes be hidden behind NDAs or orders not to tell people things."

She nodded. "In the future you'll tell me that there are things you may not be able to tell me?"

He nodded. "Not disclosing that piece of information to you was my biggest mistake and I'm sorry."

The benefits of time and waiting. "But you did trust me enough to get me the information that I needed to know, and I very much appreciate that."

"I appreciate that you didn't tell anybody other than me this," he said with a laugh.

"But seriously," she continued. "I won't ask you to break NDAs with anybody and I won't even consider the information necessary for me to know…but…"

"Yes," he said, answering her unfinished question. "I will let you know, always, when there is an NDA, or any facsimi-

If you enjoyed *The Dreidl Disaster,*
you'll love the next book in the…

Last Girls Standing series

Book 1: *B'Nai Mitzvah Mistake*

Book 2: *The Dating Contract*

Book 3: *The Dreidl Disaster*

Available now at your favorite online retailer!

Author's Note

Origins:

In December of 2018, the Washington Capitals NHL team donated hockey sticks to a Chabad in Olney, Maryland. With the donated sticks, the Chabad made a menorah and lit it for the entire town.

I read about it with joy and excitement in an article, written by Jacob Bogage on the old DC Sports Bog. That article from Jacob Bogage and the story he told me were where the seeds of this story began.

The other parts came from conversations about Hallmark movies over the years with Rachel Wagner. I love listening to her talk about the movies and I loved seeing her reaction when I told her I was going to write a 'fixer' story.

Posts by Rabbi Yael Buchler, creator of Midrash Manicures, and by the Instagram account Hanukkah Fails inspired me. Some of the ideas for the way the Empires failed in their first attempt to create a Hanukkah event actually came from conversations I had with both of these creators.

Some of the form of this book came from years of reading romance novels that centered around an event that required an entire family of characters to return home for the holidays. This kind of book is so much fun to read because it would necessitate guest appearances from characters of all sorts who appeared in books through the series, usually an author's entire backlist. Clearly, I love those books, and I hope you love my attempt to write one of my own.

Now for the research:

Kimberly Marcus and Kenny Herzog were on call for any questions I had about Westchester Politics; anything that appears incorrect in this book is on me.

I don't know cars; whatever made it look like I do came from Pete McMahon and how he walked me through the process that would make Artur a believable car guy.

Acknowledgements

There were beginnings and endings with this book; I want to thank Sinclair Sawhney for seeing a broken writer and reminding her she could write again. I also want to thank Jane Porter, Mia Gleason, Cyndi Parent, Kelly Hunter, Meghan Farrell, Voule Walker, Helena Newton and the rest of the Tule team for making magic in the midst of medical and life chaos, and believing in me.

Marnie McMahon, Megan Walski and Felicia Grossman sat with me towards the end of this book and made sure it happened. Lisa Lin, Rebecca Crowley and Kelly Cain also read this one way too many times.

To my Tule family – Rebecca Crowley, Heather Novak, Lisa Lin, Kelly Cain, Mia Heintzelman and Denise Wheatley – I adore you all.

To the admin team of Jewish Women Talking about Romance – Meredith Schorr, Felicia Grossman, Jean Meltzer, Sara Goodman Confino and Heidi Shertok – I love you all. From strength to strength, may we all go together <3

To the Romance Schmooze Discord Server – Kol hakavod <3

To the NYC Writer discord – I adore you all. I'll be your first question any time :D

To Melanie Ting, Kelly Jamieson, Fortune Whelan, and Danica Flynn – I love being a chippy chick :D

To Isabo Kelly, Heather Lire, Cassandra Carr, and Laura Hunsacker – The Empires wouldn't exist without you and I cannot wait to see what we do next.

I want to thank all of my readers who wanted to see Artur get his happy ending; this story is for you.

To the gals behind Bythepocketful – Thank you for everything you make; the designs you send shine with artistry and heart. Thank you for my title reveal bracelets and all the things.

Thank you to the bookstagrammers and book bloggers and booktokers who've read, loved, and publicized my books. I know this takes a ton of time and you have no idea how much I appreciate the time you take :D

To the Jewish Bookstagram community in particular: thank you. Thank you. Thank you. ToZoeReadss, Bookishly Vintage, and Shaked Reads for including me in the Instagram series associated with the Jewish Heritage Month Readathon this year; you not only made an author goal happen, but you gave me a place to announce the title of this book for the first time.

To Kayla – whose posts are magic and I'm so grateful to know you <3

To Heartbound Books, Loves Sweet Arrow, The Ripped Bodice, Tropes and Trifles, MeetCute Books, Roaming Romance, Barnes and Noble in Hartsdale and Eastchester,

Novel Grounds – thank you, thank you, thank you.

To the Blue Line Deli and Donald Rosner, The Chloe Belle Foundation, and to Matthew Blittner and the Brooklyn Memorial Classic – thank you for allowing me to get to know you and the work you do.

To Janel – FINALLY!!! May the next time we see each other in person be soon <3

To Emma Barry, Noue Kirwan, and KJ Micciche – I adore all of you. I cannot wait until the next time I see each of you :D

To Marnie McMahon and Megan Walski – I am so very lucky both of you are in my life. Thank you for letting me take a flight on the Phoenix. May we soar together.

To Lucy Eden. What isn't there to say? Thank you. Thank you for being my friend and letting me ride along with you <3

To Meredith Schorr, Amanda Eliott, Felicia Grossman, and Kate Goldbeck – Thank you for having some Hanukkah fun with me. Next time it's in person :D

To Lisa Lin – you got a lot of this one too. Thank you <3 I am so lucky to know you.

To Felicia Grossman and Marnie McMahon – I leaned a *lot* on both of you with this one and it doesn't go unnoticed. I adore you both.

To Luna, Minka, Kosmos, Clara, Bailey and Lockie; thank you for the skritches, the purrs, the cuddles, and the love.

To Russ and Marisa – Thank you so much for everything. Seeing your faces at events is a joy. Thank you.

Elijah – the VIP. All the questions are for you. Seeing you grow up and succeed makes me so proud. I love you.

To Mom and Dad – this year was chaos. I had a base in the chaos because of you. I love you

And to anybody I didn't include, I adore you too. Books take a village and this one ABSOLUTELY did. Thank you.

More Books by Stacey Agdern

Friendships and Festivals series

Book 1: *Miracles and Menorahs*

Book 2: *History of Us*

Book 3: *Love and Latkes*

Available now at your favorite online retailer!

About the Author

Stacey Agdern is an award-winning former bookseller who has reviewed romance novels in multiple formats and given talks about various aspects of the romance genre. She incorporates Jewish characters and traditions into her stories so that people who grew up like she did can see themselves take center stage on the page. She lives in New York, not far from her favorite hockey team's practice facility.

Thank you for reading

The Dreidl Disaster

If you enjoyed this book, you can find more from all our great authors at TulePublishing.com, or from your favorite online retailer.

TULE
PUBLISHING